Todd + Mark,

It is so awesome to see you guys again! We need to hang out SOON!

Andrew

Dedication

This book is dedicated in loving memory

to my friend,

"Sean Ford"

Forgotten Letters of the Dead

ASA PUBLISHING CORPORATION
AN INNOVATIVE OUTSOURCE BOOK PUBLISHING HYBRID

ASA Publishing Corporation
1285 N. Telegraph Rd., #376, Monroe, Michigan 48162
An Accredited Publishing House with the BBB
www.asapublishingcorporation.com

Copyrights©2019 Andrew Teague McCollister, All Rights Reserved
Book Title: Forgotten Letters of the Dead
Date Published: 02.05.2019 / Edition 1 *Trade Paperback*
Book ID: ASAPCID2380767
ISBN: 978-1-946746-50-4
Library of Congress Cataloging-in-Publication Data

This book was published in the United States of America.
Great State of Michigan

Table of Contents

-Short Stories-

Preface

For those of you who have read my first book "Beneath the Surface," I'd like to warmly welcome you back to the workings of my mind and thank you for your continued support. For those of you reading one of my publications for the first time, I'm excited to have you here and I truly hope you enjoy what I have to offer.

For those returning to my work, you'll notice "Forgotten Letters of the Dead" is a different beast from "Beneath the Surface." Where "Beneath the Surface" focused strictly on main character Conner Mills as he navigated through life and self-discovery, "Forgotten Letters of the Dead" is comprised of 10 individual tales; each of which is unrelated and highly unique.

One thing I have noticed about being a published

author is that my writing serves as an excellent conversation starter. When I say I'm an accountant, my company forces a smile before seeking refuge with my orchestral conductor boyfriend or other creative type next to me. When I say I'm a writer, I better manage to hold people's attention. This is both a good and bad thing. Good, because I love talking to people and making new friends. Bad, because it often prompts many questions, some of which I'm hesitant to answer.

People love to ask "What do you write?" It's a friendly question, but one I don't know how to answer. I could say I'm a fiction writer, but does that mean I can never publish the memoirs I've always desired to write? I could say I wrote about a character discovering their sexual identity, but would that mean all my characters have to have a comparable struggle? Writing, much like life, is filled with many paths, and people rarely follow just one road. There are twists, detours, and crabwalks we experience throughout our journeys. I personally have always struggled staying on a straight path (pun somewhat intended). I want my writing to be reflexive of real life, and that means exploring many different pathways.

As you may have realized, I'm the guy who asks the waiter for ten different recommendations before saying "screw it" and choosing the buffet. In a sense, that's what I did with this collection. That's not to say that I just threw random stories together, but rather that I attempted to create a buffet for my readers to feast upon.

The stories compiled in "Forgotten Letters of the Dead" are not constrained to a specific genre, character type, or even perspective. When embarking through this collection, I don't want you to have your experience defined by expectations. Instead, I want you to have an open mind and find that story (or stories) that really resonates with you; be it a tale of loss, fantasy, grit, or something else entirely. Who is to say what you will find after reading my collection? My only hope is that you enjoy the journey.

I realize I may have sparked more questions regarding "Forgotten Letters of the Dead." *Why is "Forgotten Letters of the Dead" your title story? Which one of your works is your favorite? Do you relate with any of the characters? Why is zero divided by zero undefined?*

These are questions to which I actually do have an answer: Read the book and see what you find...

Forgotten Letters
of the Dead

Mr. Cinnamon

When revisiting my childhood, the memories I recall most fondly were those of my mother. I remember the stories she told me before she became president of the neighborhood watch. At night, once I was nestled under my warm silk covers, she entered, sometimes in her work suit but more often than not in a night robe. She read several different stories, but my favorites were the ones she made up. She spun many tales about shy unicorns and clever mice, but none were quite as special as . . .

"The Lonely Spider," she said. Her enthusiasm was detectable to even a nine-year old's ears. The words erupted from mother with such speed and power that nothing was left trapped in the newly forming wrinkles around her jawline.

"There once was a spider who lived in the tallest oak tree in the forest."

"Do spiders live in oak trees?"

"This spider does. She lived in the largest, leafiest tree in the entire magical forest. But it was also the loneliest tree in the forest. Though the spider spent most of her day knitting different blankets from her silk for the many guests she often dreamed would visit, no one ever came."

"One day, the spider decided she was tired of waiting for someone to visit. She packed her finest silk blanket and traveled to the neighboring willow tree. There she found a large group of flies playing with each other. As the spider watched the many flies laughing and playing amongst themselves, she grew very happy. She longed to have a playmate to laugh with as well. The spider examined each of the flies until she found the smallest, most beautiful fly she could find. Everything about him was perfect, except he wouldn't stop shaking."

"The spider asked the fly why he continued to shake.

The fly told the spider that he was cold, and nothing ever seemed to be able to warm him. Upon hearing this, the spider took him in her silk blanket and wrapped him up tight for warmth."

At this time, mother pulled my covers up under my chin and tucked the folds tight under my arms. "The young fly was so grateful, that he agreed to come live with the spider. From then on, the spider and the fly played and laughed together every day and snuggled together under the spider's warm blankets at night. The fly no longer needed to shake, and the spider was never lonely again."

"Why does the spider want a fly friend?" I asked.

"So she won't be lonely anymore."

"But don't spiders eat flies?"

"Most do, but this spider wanted to be special."

"I think it should be a baby spider, not a fly."

"This spider wanted a fly," Mom said. However, she eventually conceded to my demands. The shaking fly became a shaking spider. Mom continued to tell me the story, but her words lost just a touch of enthusiasm. The deflation wasn't evident at the time. It was so slight, in fact, that I don't believe my mother consciously recognized it.

***

Growing up, names were never my strength. Remembering a name was challenging because it was independent of an individual's physical appearance and character. It was illogical that a sweet little girl in my old class could be called something as menacing as Brunnhilda while the strictest teacher on the school grounds was referred to as Ms. Flower. Rather than names, I tended to remember faces and prescribe more fitting titles.

After my mother and I moved from the city to the suburbs, I became involved with a trio of classmates. As with most groups, there was a de-facto leader. Ours was Stephen. He was about two inches shorter than me, but the assertive way he carried himself made me feel as if I should slouch. Even at the age of fourteen, the curly black hair on his head was matched by fewer, but equally curly chest hairs protruding from the top collar of his shirt. These traits led me to refer to him as Bear.

Marcus was Bear's right hand. He shared many traits with a common turtle. He expressed a tough exterior, but was withdrawn. This character trait wasn't the result of insecurity, but rather a lack of interest in the rest of the world. I'd further classify him as a snapping turtle. On two hands I could count the number of times he spoke directly to me, none of which were particularly inviting.

Out of the group, I probably felt the closest to Rabbit. He was especially appealing to me because I was able to call him Rabbit to his face. Bear and Turtle assigned the nickname years before we met. While I didn't peg either one as creative geniuses, the name was a good fit. He spoke less than Turtle and seemed almost timid when others approached too quickly. His physical appearance matched as well. He was just slightly overweight with soft brown hair and a pale but welcoming face. He sported a small flattened nose which would even twitch from time to time due to his allergies. I was never able to remember his real name. If I had to guess, I would say it started with an H. Harold? Maybe Henry?

I first met Bear in our school parking lot. I was tying my shoe when a grey minivan pulled up to the curve. A woman quickly exited the car and ran to the other side to usher her son out. The woman seized the boy's shirt collar and began vigorously contorting it. I'll never forget the look on Bear's face, because it was the only time I ever witnessed it. The confidence that tirelessly layered itself around him was transparent as he half-heartedly struggled against his mother's grooming.

The woman continued to battle with her son until her eyes made contact with me. "You just moved here, didn't you?" She released her son's collar and made her way towards me. She told me her name, but I don't remember it. The woman who stood before me was tall, thin, and had blond hair pulled tightly into a bun. She was cloaked in a pungent perfume which failed to mask the coffee beans on her breath.

"My name's Duncan." I smiled.

My hand was clenched in a firm shake. "It is a pleasure meeting you. Stephen, why don't you invite Duncan over? If we kidnap him, maybe his mom will have to come to one of our meetings."

I tried to reach a consensus on what was just said to me, but before I could, Coffee Bean Woman was in the car and the minivan was on the road.

"Hey," I said.

He nodded.

"What meeting was your mom talking about?"

Bear sighed. "She runs our neighborhood's security committee." I wasn't sure if his annoyance stemmed from his mother's position or my question.

I laughed, nervously. "Why do we need a security committee?"

Bear eyed me, suddenly intrigued. "You haven't heard of Mr. Cimeno?"

Bear brought me to his group after class. I assumed Bear was giving me the honor of introducing myself, which is why he didn't initiate an introduction.

"Hey, I'm Duncan." I extended my arm towards Turtle. He looked confused for a moment. This confusion must have been taxing because he barely had the energy to extend his arm. Rabbit took my hand quickly. If possible, his handshake was limper than Turtle's.

"So, I hear we all live in the same neighborhood." I was just hearing about this guy on our street, Mr. Cinnamon

. . ." I stopped talking.

Turtle scrunched his face. "Who?"

I couldn't believe I did that. I couldn't remember the guy's name. He lived by himself on the edge of the woods and his name sounded like Cinnamon, that's all I knew.

"He's talking about Joseph Cimeno, the pedophile." Bear said.

"Yeah, it's crazy. Apparently my mom and I moved into the house across the street from him."

"It's not that crazy. There are perverts and pedos everywhere." Turtle said.

"Shut up, asshole," Bear said. It comforted me to see that Bear assigned names to people as well. "Duncan here has a front row seat to the action." He put his arm around my shoulder. "I've always wanted to sneak into the guy's house, see what kind of weird shit he's hiding. You, my man, can be our lookout. Tell us when he's not there."

As I walked home from school that day, I took the opportunity to inspect Mr. Cinnamon's home. Three of its four sides were surrounded by trees. Behind the home, a vast line of forestry extended beyond my line of sight. It was as if the woods had opened up to reveal the house to the world. Other than that, it actually looked relatively normal. I noticed he had long draped curtains, the kind you read about in Victorian literature.

When I arrived home, mother greeted me with a smile. "How was school today?"

I told her that I made some friends. "That sounds wonderful. Are they nice?"

"Mom, is it true a pedophile lives across the street? Mr. Cinnamon?" Mom was accustomed to my name assignments.

"Nothing's been proven. He's just a man who's a little strange. People love to spread stories about anyone who doesn't conform to what they deem as normal." She rolled her eyes. "That security woman had him made out to be a common criminal."

"Coffee Bean Woman? Her son is one of my new friends. She wants you to join her security group."

"Oh, she is so annoying. She's been here twice already trying to get me to join that stupid neighborhood watch. She told me all about Mr. Cimeno, *the big bad danger to our way of life*. She doesn't know if he's really been convicted of anything. It's just a rumor she's using to make herself feel important."

"She seemed nice to me."

"A lot of people seem nice, Duncan. A group like that wouldn't understand me." I recognized the look on my mother's face. Emotionally I didn't comprehend what it meant but I knew it as the look she always gave when discussing the manner of my birth.

That night mom tucked me into bed. As per tradition, she told me the story of The Lonely Spider.

***

I saw Mr. Cinnamon the next morning. I was walking to school. I just finished waving bye to mom as she tended to her garden when I heard a humming coming from Mr. Cinnamon's house. He was sitting atop a riding lawnmower.

Mr. Cinnamon was tall and of average build, not skinny but not fat. The day was cloudy. It seemed appropriate that he would tend to his lawn. His skin was pale to the extent that I wasn't sure if it had ever had direct contact with sunlight. I thought about what Mom said about him not fitting in with the neighborhood. I waved to him. He waved back.

In class, I watched as everyone found their *correct* groups. The cheerleaders, jocks, cool kids, uncool kids . . . I didn't need to join them, I already had Bear's group. Growing up I longed to be part of a group. Ever since I was old enough to care what others thought of me, I cared about being accepted.

I found Rabbit sitting in the cafeteria. He briefly flashed a smile before returning to his meal. I found myself contemplating my words before I spoke. They needed to be strategically delivered in order to shatter his silence.

"I saw Mr. C . . . the pedophile today. He didn't seem too scary."

"I'd be careful. My dad's a cop, he said there're some registered sex offenders in the area."

"What?" My shock stemmed more from hearing Rabbit talk. I realized that I hadn't heard him speak until that moment. His voice was quiet, coming from his breath more than vocal cords. "Can you ask him to look up who they are?"

"I don't know. I don't see him much since he and Mom divorced."

I told him I was sorry. I thought about telling him about my father, or lack thereof. I reasoned that revealing that I was a test-tube baby would be an embarrassment for my mother. She always said people had more respect for a single mother abandoned than a single mother by choice. However, in truth my silence wasn't for her. Even years later after my mother's eventual passing, I avoided the topic of my father, only referring to my artificial origin as a last resort.

Rabbit opened his mouth to speak again but stopped as Bear and Turtle joined us. "Dude, what's wrong with your mom?" I looked at him. *Was he talking to me?* "Duncan, your mom is so rude. My mom offered her a spot on the neighborhood security watch. She said the door was practically slammed in her face."

"I'm sorry about that. I don't think she meant offense. She just doesn't think the security watch is necessary."

"Of course it is! Did you not hear us talking about

Mr. Cimeno? You shouldn't believe all the crazy stories your mom tells you."

On my way back from school, I found my eyes wandering towards Mr. Cinnamon's house. Something felt different. I couldn't put my finger on it. My mind was already racing. *Could what Bear and Rabbit talked about be true? Was I really living across the street from a pedophile?* Then I noticed. The curtains! One of them was pulled back. It was slight, not enough to see in but more than enough to see out. Rationalizing my feeling was impossible, but I knew Mr. Cinnamon was peering out of the curtain. He was gazing at the outside world. He was gazing at me. When I realized I had stopped walking, I quickly turned my head and continued towards my house.

At night, Mom tucked me into bed. I stopped her before she could begin the story. "Mom, is it ok if I go to bed without a story tonight?"

She nodded. "I was starting to think you were getting too old. We don't need to do story time anymore."

"We don't have to stop, just not every night." I said.

"Honestly, the way you like to tell it is kind of weird. Spiders don't play with flies."

She hid her pain so well. The illusion of transparency my mother portrayed still fascinates me. It wasn't until her funeral, that I realized what the story truly meant to her. It wasn't just a story. It was *her* story, *our* story. She was the lonely spider and I was her shaking fly.

***

Every morning, Mr. Cinnamon would leave his house almost precisely when I would leave for school. I would notice his car entering the driveway nearly half an hour after I returned. Monday was a half day. My opportunity was in sight.

I presented my plan to my friends at school. They were so intently listening to my words, that none of them tried to interrupt or even say anything at all.

"He comes home every day at 3:00. I've seen him. This is our chance! We can sneak into his house and find evidence about what he's done. If he really is what everyone thinks he is, then there has to be something there that will prove it."

I waited for their questions. I anticipated numerous

objections to my proposal. However, I was prepared with a counter to any and all concerns. *How will we get inside?* The front door. I'd seen Mr. Cinnamon return home multiple times. He always paused to lift up the fake rock on his porch before opening the door. He must keep a key under there. *What if he comes back early?* He wouldn't. But just in case, we would have the people not entering the house stand watch. *What if someone else sees us going into the house?* That wouldn't happen either. Every adult would be at work. I was prepared for anything. Anything except for the silence I received.

Obviously, they were still digesting my plan. That is what I kept telling myself. Finally Bear growled an exhausted grunt. "You do you, man," he said, shaking his head.

I could tell he was annoyed, but I didn't understand why. He was the one always talking about exposing the pedophile on our street. *Was I not supposed to take him seriously?* My mother didn't, and he had no trouble making fun of her for it.

I tried to voice my plan's need for watchmen, but

the words wouldn't form. *Why was it that I was less afraid about breaking into a potential pedophile's house, than actually saying what was on my mind?* I never had trouble speaking my mind in the past. Before we moved, I was always boisterous and confident. I left without furthering my presentation. I was determined to infiltrate Mr. Cinnamon's house on my own. I couldn't explain it, but somehow I knew he held the key to figuring out what was wrong with me.

***

Facing the gingerbread house (it took me a while to devise the perfect name for Mr. Cinnamon's home) was less daunting than I thought. My brain was swirling with so many thoughts, that there was no room for fear. The wind was blowing harder than usual today. I shielded my face with my sleeve as I crossed his lawn.

I found the fake rock quickly. With all the plants and natural life he had around his home, it stuck out like a sore thumb. However, when I lifted it, I found no key. Instead, there was a small, slightly crumpled bag. It felt mushy, like sand. I examined it closely and discovered it was plant fertilizer.

Slightly confused but mostly annoyed, I placed the bag carefully back under the false boulder. I needed to think. *How would I enter a gingerbread house?* My first instinct was naturally the front door, but that was no longer a viable option. *The windows!* In most stories they were made of peppermint. A few good licks would wear them down. Clearly I knew Mr. Cinnamon's windows weren't actually made of peppermint, but they were still an option worth investigating.

When I reached the front window, I gasped. The curtains were moving. For a moment it looked like Mr. Cinnamon was pulling them back to spy on the world. I took a moment to breathe and realized it was only the wind. *Maybe Mr. Cinnamon wasn't actually watching me? Though last time I walked by, I could have sworn I saw his fingers.* Regardless, curtains moving meant an open window, which also meant I had my entrance.

The window led to a relatively normal kitchen. There were a few more plants than usual, but besides that nothing was really out of the ordinary. It was slightly messy with some dirty dishes stacked in the sink. There were no pictures of naked children, just a small round dining table set for four. I imagined he didn't use the extra seats much.

I shivered. The wind was picking up now. I closed the window and latched it shut. I needed to remember to open it before I left.

I wondered what the guys would say when I told them how normal the house looked. Honestly, they'd probably say I didn't look hard enough. I'd try to insist that I did, but they wouldn't listen, and I'd give up. My mind started swirling again. *Why was I having so much trouble saying what was on my mind?* Before I moved to the suburbs and met Bear, Turtle, and Rabbit, I wasn't like that. In the city I shared all my thoughts and people listened. I bet Bear couldn't make it into the house on his own. He probably wouldn't have given my idea to check the window a second thought.

I was almost amazed at my own brilliance. Sure, it didn't take a genius to know window equals entrance. But Mom always said that true intelligence wasn't always having the right answer, it was knowing when to look for a new one. It was just like the story she used to tell me about the mouse who, after discovering the kitchen was littered with mouse traps, convinced the family cat that . . .

I stopped. That was it. The issue wasn't the location, the people, or even Mr. Cinnamon. I did the math incorrectly. It wasn't an addition problem, it was a subtraction problem. I'd lost something. "Her stories," I whispered.

If I thought people were judging me, I thought of the shy unicorn. She thought the horses wouldn't accept her because of her horn, until the day she used it to save them from a hungry fox. During the days I felt inadequate, I remembered the clever mouse. He tricked the cat into thinking he was torturing him by bringing him all the cheese he could eat. When I felt lonely, I thought of the lonely spider and the shaking fly.

Suddenly, I heard something. It sounded like someone screaming. No, it wasn't screaming. It was breaks. Car breaks. Mr. Cinnamon! He did come back early!

I didn't think, I only reacted. I dove behind the curtain. I tried to unlatch the window, but my hands were shaking too hard. I tried to steady them. They started sweating so badly, I couldn't even grip the handle. Soon, it was too late. The front door slammed open. My heart sank.

"What a day," I heard him sigh. His voice was soothing, but not sweet. I waited for him to say more, but instead I only heard clinking. It sounded like he was setting the table. *Was he going to cook? Maybe he would need to leave the room for something?* It was almost worse for me to think about running through the house and accidently running into him. *Maybe I could get the window open?* I just needed him to leave so he wouldn't hear me.

The clanking of pots stopped. I could feel the silence. I could feel him standing still, staring at something. But what?

"You look thirsty, Duncan. May I offer you a drink?"

People say when you meet the love of your life, time stands still. I know that isn't true. It is when you feel sheer terror beyond anything you ever thought possible, that time truly stops. I've felt this sensation twice in my life. Once when my wife told me she was pregnant. The other time was when I was crouched behind the curtain of Mr.

Cinnamon's window, moments after he spoke my name.

I waited for him to approach me. I heard his feet shuffling around the kitchen. *He's going to rip the curtain open. He's going to find me. I'll be chained up in his basement. Years later when he's done with me, he'll mail the pictures he took of me to my Mom.*

"You look thirsty as well, Abigail and Jasmine. Join us."

Were there others? When I finally worked up the courage, I peeked through the hole. Mr. Cinnamon was sitting around his dining table with three potted plants seated in the other chairs.

"I made sure yours was warm, Jasmine. Just the way you like it." He poured a glass of steaming water into what looked like a planter full of oversized green peas. I later discovered that particular plant was called a Java Fern.

"Here you go Abigail." He poured a second glass into a broad-leafed plant seated across the table.

"And I didn't forget you, Duncan. I brought two shots for you as usual." He poured two glasses into the banana plant seated next to him. "I need one myself." He chugged a glass of something that wasn't water.

"The client's been giving me hell again," Mr. Cinnamon spoke in a matter-of-fact manner with a slight grin that suggested annoyance. "The same one as before." He paused. I couldn't tell if he was recalling the event or imagining the plants responding to him.

Most others would've seen a madman. I did find him strange, but I also had sympathy for him. He wasn't plotting to kidnap me, he was talking about his plant. A satisfied smile stretched across my face. I waited only a little longer before Mr. Cinnamon excused himself. When I heard the kitchen door slam, I threw back the curtain and made a dash for the door.

I stopped just short of the kitchen table. *I needed something. No one would believe me if I didn't have proof.* It had to be something significant, something fast. The Duncan plant caught my eye. It seemed smaller than other banana plants I'd seen. With a shudder, a thought came to mind. *Did he get this plant before or after I moved to the neighborhood?*

A floor board creaked. I seized Duncan and ran out

of the house.

***

I called the gang to my room. Bear and Turtle sat on my bed, leaving me and Rabbit standing. I told them about my voyage through Mr. Cinnamon's manor. I thrust my arms through the air as I expressed how he treated his plants like people. I held up Duncan and pointed to him. I noticed Bear and Turtle looked at each other more than they looked at me. I lowered my voice as if somehow it would help me recapture their attention. When I was finished my voice was half as loud as when I started. We sat in uncomfortable silence for a while.

"Either you're lying or you're stupid." Turtle spoke in a low dry voice, using a minimum amount of effort for each of his words.

"Yeah," Bear said. "So he talks to plants, that doesn't prove he doesn't kidnap people. Mr. Cimeno will probably know you took the plant that he named after you. Good luck with that."

Bear and Turtle got up to leave. I tried to think of what to say, but nothing came to mind. Rabbit stayed behind. Once the others were out of my room he spoke in a quiet whispery voice. "They didn't have the courage to do what you did."

"Thanks," I said. I looked down at Duncan and ran my fingers slowly up his stem.

"Why did you take that plant?" He said slightly more confidently.

"I don't know. I needed proof and he might have named it after me. I guess . . ." I looked back up at Rabbit. Our eyes met. "Maybe I just wanted someone to talk to."

Rabbit didn't look surprised. Instead he gave a slight nod, which may have indicated he felt the same way. Then he turned and ran outside to catch up with the others.

I kept Duncan for nine days. Nine days I watered the plant and placed it in the window for sunlight. My window that faced our backyard. That was important. I didn't want Mr. Cinnamon to see it.

Through my front yard window, I watched for Mr. Cinnamon. I didn't go out with Bear, Turtle, or Rabbit. Mr. Cinnamon was nowhere to be seen. I didn't see him taking out the trash or getting his morning paper. I didn't notice his curtain pulled back. *He wasn't even spying.* One night I thought I heard the sound of lawnmower engine. I sprang from my bed and flung open my curtains expecting to see Mr. Cinnamon mowing his lawn in the dead of night. Instead, I witnessed one of the neighborhood high school girls stumbling quietly from her car to her front porch and mouthing curse words as she dropped her keys.

"Where could he be?" I said. "He has to have noticed. Is he hiding from me? Or is he not going outside because I'm not there?" I gasped and threw my hand over my mouth when I realized I was talking to Duncan.

I ran to the other window and seized the plant. I intended to shake it. I wanted to beat the answers out of it. Smash it against the wall, if necessary. Then, I noticed something. A black dot on the plant, like a mole. But it was moving rapidly. It was a spider. A spider had made a web on Duncan! There was something in its web, cradled in a silk blanket. A fly!

I ran to my front window. I looked in my yard and saw Mom tending to her garden. The feeling that came over me was strange. It was a mixture of excitement and nostalgia. I had to show her. She needed to see it. We needed to see it together. I ran down the stairs to the front door. I opened the front down and ran across our front porch looking for Mom. I didn't see her. But what I did see, staring at me from across the street was Mr. Cinnamon.

With one foot on our walkway and the other on the porch step, I stood motionless. I was confident the boiling cement was burning my bare foot, but I couldn't feel it. My body went numb, incapable of feeling or movement of any kind.

He stared for a moment longer, then opened his mouth slightly and nodded in realization. He stepped closer. His face scrunched tightly together as if focusing on a single target, me. Contempt spread like a lethal injection across the chapped craters of his face as he drew near. Then, with only a few feet separating us, I noticed he was smiling. It was slight, but so sudden that I gasped.

"Can I help you," Mom's voice was cracked but firm. She stood between me and Mr. Cinnamon, clenching her hand securely into my shoulder blade.

This seemed to startle Mr. Cinnamon. He twitched

backward, the smile revoked. I peered up past my mother's cut-off jeans at the man who was now halfway up our lawn. He stared at Mom with more confusion than anything else.

He turned abruptly. For a moment, I thought he was going to leave. Then he snapped back around and extended a long, crooked finger at me. "The plant." The voice was much deeper than what I heard in his house.

A thousand fire ants could've burrowed their teeth into every inch of my body and I wouldn't have noticed. I wanted to give him the plant. I wanted to throw myself at his mercy and beg for his forgiveness. I wanted to, but as my mother's grip tightened on my shoulder, so did mine on Duncan.

"You need to make sure you water it twice a day." In a casual manner, he turned around and left our yard. Mom ushered me inside. I didn't look back.

***

Standing on my front porch cradling Duncan's silk covered body was the last time I saw Mr. Cinnamon in person. "My mom said he snuck out in the middle of the night," Bear told our group. "That means he captured another kid for his collection. He's off to the next neighborhood now."

"I say good riddance," Bear's mother said after rather loudly sipping her tea. She was more proper than I remembered from the parking lot, wearing evening shoes and a Sunday dress to Wednesday afternoon tea with my mother. Ever since the day Mr. Cinnamon visited our front yard, my mom and Coffee Bean Woman began having regular tea days. Soon other moms started coming over. It wasn't long before every Saturday Mom would spend the early mornings in the kitchen baking cookies, chocolate cake, or some other pastry for her weekly security club meetings.

The women stayed for hours laughing about things I didn't understand. They seemed more interested in gossiping about who was sleeping with whom than about actual security risks. Mom told me to not worry about what they were doing and go play with my friends.

I told mom, I wanted to continue with story time. She tried, I truly believe she did, but something was missing. There just wasn't passion to her words anymore.

I encouraged her to continue. We discussed new story ideas. I waited up night after night for her to enter my bedroom, renewed, and tell me her stories. The stories that gave me the confidence to be who I needed to be. More and more nights I went without, until she finally said, "Do you think Stephen still waits up at night for his mom to read him bedtime stories?"

"You don't have to read to me. Just tell me a story. Tell me about the Lonely Spider."

"You know the story already."

"Then you can change it." I told her it didn't have to be a shaking spider anymore. It could be a fly.

"Don't be silly," she said. "Spiders play with spiders, not flies."

***

I didn't think about Joseph Cimeno until almost twenty years later. I was reading through the newspaper when his name caught my eye in the obituary section. The article was short, stating only that he worked as a computer technician following a short career as an environmental teacher and was survived by three nephews. It mentioned nothing about him being a sex offender.

That night, as per tradition, I went into my son's room. I asked him what bedtime story he wanted to hear. He responded with a stereotypical shrug with an accompaniment of twirling his curly blond hair. My wife didn't like the stories I told him. I believe it was fifth on the list of reasons why she eventually left.

"I have a new one for tonight," I said. He bit his lip eagerly awaiting its commencement. "It's called Mr. Cinnamon."

"Mr. Cinnamon lived on Peppermint street. As one would suspect, all the houses on Peppermint street were made of the richest, most pure peppermint sticks imaginable. The only house that wasn't made from peppermint belonged to Mr. Cinnamon. He lived in a house made of gingerbread. There was a rumor that if you knocked three times on Mr. Cinnamon's front door, he would appear and give you the most delicious gingerbread man in the world."

"However, no one ever knocked on Mr. Cinnamon's door. You see, there was another rumor about Mr.

Cinnamon. According to this rumor, if Mr. Cinnamon caught you setting foot on his property he would chain you up in his basement and not feed you until you agreed to be his elf slave. There were claims that he had three elf slaves already: Duncan, Abigail, and Jasmine. They were three school children who at one point or another dared to knock on his door. Everyone was too afraid that the second rumor was the true one, so Mr. Cinnamon never received any visitors."

My boy ceased turning his hair between his fingers and sat upright, enthused by my words. "Did anyone ever try to visit him?" He asked.

"Eventually, a group of four young boys decided to brave Mr. Cinnamon's doorstep. They were only a few years older than you." I gently flicked my son's nose. He giggled slightly before brushing my hand away.

"Their names were Bear, Turtle, Rabbit, and Fly. Fly was the smallest of his friends, but he was also the wisest and carried himself with outspoken confidence. Fly was the group's leader."

Salty Air

I shut my eyes and let my toes curl into the earth. It was a warm day, but the sand felt cold and clumped beneath my feet. It probably rained earlier. A deep breath allowed me to take in the bitter salty air. In the distance, I could hear the gentle roar of the waves crashing into the jagged rocks. It was so astounding how something as powerful as a wave could treat something as rough as a rock, with such ease and tenderness.

I suppose that is how the ocean has always cared for its creatures. It molded itself to fit the needs of anything and everything that wanted to be a part of it. It cradled all its life with the soothing touch of a mother holding a newborn. It *slowly rocked back and forth those above while providing warmth and comfort to those below.*

I held your hand and together we walked. Your footprints were uneven and every so often a large circular indention marked your loss of balance. When you were too tired to walk, I carried you. On the way back to our tent, I entered the water and let your feet stroke its surface. It was cold, and you shivered. You shirked and claimed you hated the sea.

Eventually, you grew fond of the ocean; some days surfing its tides, while others rocking in its waves. You were sad when we moved to the mountains. You thought life would end without the warm embrace of sand hugging your ankles. Nothing could match the sensation of salty water freely flowing through your hair. However, soon the crisp mountain air became your new oasis.

You spent many days exploring the new terrain. The breeze surrounded you, causing the leaves to dance. They swayed, but never relinquished the gentle grip of the tree branches. This gave you peace of mind. Hiking through the rocky trail made your legs grow strong. Swimming through the mountain river matured your body. You were the embodiment of manhood; no one ever denied it.

I cried when you left. Your future stretched beyond what I could offer. I knew this but couldn't contain my emotion.

The graduation cap and diploma clung to your body with such ease, many would assume them to be extra appendages. You commanded presence with your speech. Many were moved to tears, me being no exception. Your words graciously flowed from your lips like a mockingbird singing to its children. You congratulated your friends and thanked your professors. The final words being unyielding gratitude for me.

Years following your graduation, you returned to our beach. This time, you held a hand that wasn't mine. You glided across the sand. With poise and grace, you lowered yourself to one knee.

I watched from the sand dunes. I knew what you were asking her. You told me to let you take this next step on your own. I respected your wishes but couldn't resist bearing witness to this moment. You were so beautiful;

smiling as the sun's rays illuminated every crevice of your body.

Tears filled her eyes, as you slid the ring on her trembling finger. I knew she loved you, but she would never be able to fully comprehend the sheer volume of tenderness and joy you would bestow on her life.

Years later, my hand clenched a tiny jumble of fingers. My skin was tight and patched with wrinkles, but my stride was steady and smooth. The young boy's footprints were uneven and every so often, he lost his balance . . .

***

The sun was high in the sky, barely progressing past its typical noon placement. In the center of the desolate beach, Tina Marie stood mere inches from the crashing waves. She wore professional attire. Neither her facial expression nor body language expressed concern for her expensive wardrobe being so near a large body of water. Any who knew the woman would find this uncustomary. She massaged the center of her flat stomach, as if by habit.

A man approached her. He was tall, slender, and on

most days carried himself with confidence. He hadn't asked his wife why this particular beach was so important. In fact, he hadn't raised a single question or comment to her the entire trip.

The man eyed the letter clenched in his wife's palm. Since her doctor's visit the prior week, she hadn't spoken more than necessary. His wife had spent several sleepless nights in her study, hunched over that letter amidst the dim glow of a solitary desk lamp. The specialist recommended she write to the child. The creature would never take a breath. Only two weeks ago did they even discover it was male, yet he was her confidant. More than anything, the man longed to read his wife's words. His desire solely focused on knowing the thoughts she couldn't share with him.

A light wind whispered through the sand dunes. Though the day was warm, the woman shook. She dangled the paper before her unbreaking gaze. With no visible signs of hesitance or remorse, she shredded the note. Her hand uncoiled and the pieces flew into the sea.

She watched the scattered ashes of her unborn child

intermix with the salty water. Sandy footprints, clinging caps and gowns, a trembling ring finger . . . the fragments of his untold story were dissolving into the dark abyss.

Instinctively, the man charged into the water; attempting to secure the pieces before the liquid rendered them illegible. The woman closed her eyes. She caressed her stomach with large, repetitive circles.

At first, she could only hear her husband, splashing in the distance. However, soon the noise was replaced by a different sound. At first it appeared faint, but gradually grew. Suddenly, she recognized the voice. A boy was crying. She extended her hand; perhaps to comfort or perhaps to distance herself.

Then she opened her eyes and saw only air.

A Moon Among Stars

"My son is going to change the world." My mother always said these words before tucking me into bed. It took place after she parted my hair and before her warm lips pressed against my forehead.

After my father left, she started including everyone in the ritual. Every teacher at my school, parent in my neighborhood, and store owner within a five-mile radius of our house heard about her son, "the future miracle worker."

I didn't mean to keep disappointing Mom. It just

happened.

High school was the worst. During my junior year, a freshman named Charlie Almond disappeared for three days. The entire town erupted into panic until his return. Afterwards, school didn't seem very exciting. I took it upon myself to change that.

History class was so boring. The professor, Mr. Howard I think his name was, spoke in a monotone. He tended to ramble about unimportant details such as the types of wigs during the colonial period. And it was always without any inflection.

One day, I asked a classmate named Sally to tell Mr. Howard what she really thought of him. Sally was a quiet girl; the kind that sat in the back of class, never raising her hand. Mr. Howard's face was priceless when she stood before the class and called him "A shit breath old coot."

Unfortunately, I forgot to tell Sally not to mention I gave her the idea. Mom was furious. For the rest of the school year she made me clean Mr. Howard's car every Friday and do all of Sally's weekend chores.

Some might call my mother harsh, but she had a soft

side. She only grounded me for two months when I dared the class valedictorian to moon the principal. I'm sure she secretly thought it was funny when he got detention. Even the parents knew he was a suck up.

I knew I didn't really have to listen to Mom, but I always did. I accepted any punishment she ever gave me. I never talked back to her, not since I was six.

I wanted to make Mom proud. I dedicated myself to becoming a surgeon. I took up community service after class. I tried so hard not to fall into temptation again. For a while, I was successful.

I didn't lose control when I failed my first Chemistry test or when my car was impounded for parking illegally. I didn't even lose it when my only high school girlfriend cheated on me with another girl. I did however, eventually give in to the pressure. Though I'm still not exactly sure why it happened the way it did.

Most medical colleges wanted incoming students to have internship experience. My Physics professor arranged a phone interview with a local surgeon he knew from church. I felt uncharacteristically nervous when I asked to shadow at his practice. "That sounds fine," he said in a voice more mechanical than the dial tone. "Come by tomorrow, and my wife will get you set up. She handles the business end."

The thing I remember most about his building was the weight of the front door. I imagined people would require surgery after trying to push it open. I also didn't count on how hard the door would slam once I let go. The small waiting room lit up as people turned to face the source of the commotion.

It wasn't long before a young blonde woman stepped out of an almost unnoticeable corner office. "You must be Glenn," she said with a voice slightly higher than what I expected. "Come this way."

She closed the door once I was inside. Her office was small and filled with pictures of her with a long faced, much older looking man I assumed to be her husband. "I'm Mrs. Hatcher," she said. She extended her arm and clenched mine in a firm handshake. "I hear your teacher is friends with my husband. Is that how you got your foot in our door?"

Her smile made my jaw cramp. I was almost a foot taller than she, but that toothy thin-lipped grin seemed to glare down at me. I squeezed her hand tighter. "How do you do, Mrs. Hatcher?"

Dr. Hatcher rarely smiled. I liked that. His voice was low and gargled with age. "A steady hand and a strong stomach are all you need for this job," he said. His hands were plastered in liver spots and wrinkles, but they were steady.

Dr. Hatcher was an ear, nose, and throat surgeon. Since blood was never my favorite part of the human anatomy, I reasoned that this line of work would be less gruesome. I quickly changed my sentiment once he removed a two-inch-thick, moist mixture of pus, hair, and bird poop from a man's ear and said it was ear wax.

I tried to focus on the helping people aspect of the job. People did appear happier once they hacked up a bucket full of congestion or were finished having a Q-tip crammed up their nose.

All in all, my first day of shadowing went well until

one man, with a chronic nose bleed, asked for my help. Dr. Hatcher had just explained to the man that he may need minor surgery to help cauterize his blood vessels on a permanent basis to stop the frequent bleeding. After that, he stepped out of the room and left me alone with the poor guy. I tried not to focus on the blood-stained tissue he applied to his nostril while he spoke. "Young man, you think this surgery is a good idea? My wife made me come here. Damn thing will probably go away with a warm rag."

I tried phrasing my answer as carefully as possible. "If it were me, I would get the surgery. It sounds like the right call."

Within moments, Mrs. Hatcher was standing in the doorway. The smiling woman didn't break eye contact as she beckoned me. *God, I hated her smile.*

"I didn't know you were going to be here for two whole hours," she said through her bitten lip. I didn't recall her setting a time limit.

"Glenn, do you know why I called you over here?"

"I'm not sure."

"I heard you giving your two cents to one of our

patients," she said. "Now I know how tempting it can be to get chit chatty with them, but remember our patients didn't come here to hear your recommendations. After all, you haven't even graduated from high school. Medical schools aren't going to take you if you continue to overstep your boundaries."

Mom made me practice my way of communication. Questions not demands, "I" not "You," lots of head nods . . . Mrs. Hatcher practiced a different way. *She honestly thought she could say whatever she wanted without consequence.* I found myself wanting to teach her a lesson.

"Why don't you head home," she said. "I'll call you and we can talk about the next time you can come observe."

I could've silenced her then. I'm not sure what stopped me. I'd like to think it was a conscience, but it was more like admiration. Don't get me wrong, I hated her. Everything about her pointed face got under my skin; her bleached blonde hair, turned up nose. And that smile . . . There was just something about the control she commanded. Perhaps she was like me?

Two weeks passed and the only calls I got were telemarketers. Each time my phone rang, I felt this rush. My blood raced to my head and pounded through my eardrum. I returned to normal when the computerized voice asked about my supply of cosmetics.

I fantasized about what Mrs. Hatcher sounded like through the phone. *I sounded weak, because I didn't have any control.* She was young, maybe seven years older than me. Her voice was high. So, I bet she sounded younger, more powerful. I knew I had to call her. It could be dangerous. Somehow, I needed to convince her to see me in person.

A bubbly, "Hello," rang into my ear. She sounded calm, but in a piercing way. It was slight, but I noticed the shift in tone when Mrs. Hatcher heard my voice. "Oh Glenn, I was getting ready to call you. Why don't you come in tomorrow? Say 12-1. We can make it a once a week thing. Will that satisfy you?"

It was easy to hear the contempt. *Well played, Mrs. Hatcher.* I knew that 12-1 the office was closed for lunch, so I would most likely just be cleaning up after the doctors. It definitely wouldn't give me enough hours to pass my course. "That sounds great! When should I stop by?"

"We'll talk about that in person tomorrow," she said. "Try not to be late, remember punctuality is a professional courtesy." I heard the phone click.

I should've been more worried about passing my internship, or about the lack of surgical experience I was receiving, but I wasn't. I was only fixated on her. It was probably then, that I realized I didn't care to be a surgeon.

The second the door crashed behind me, Mrs. Hatcher's head poked from her office. She smiled as she reeled me in with her finger. There were no patients and most of the staff was on break, but she still shut the door behind me.

I let her make the first move . . .

"I understand you want some more hours, Glenn." She raised her beckoning finger and slightly tilted her head. "One thing students seem to have trouble understanding is that this is a serious business and not a social hour. We are more than happy to help you out, but I think you can agree we've gone above and beyond . . ."

"Stop talking," I said.

As always, it happened instantly. She didn't speak. Her lips curled until they formed a line which stretched across her face. The most chilling part was how similar it was to her regular display. I was slightly disappointed. I think I expected more of a challenge.

I fumbled through my book bag for what felt like an eternity. I avoided looking at her as much as possible. Something about the eyes always bothered me; the pupils slightly over dilated and never shifting. Finally, I found what I was looking for.

I handed her my hours sheet and a pencil. "Take these," I said. "Fill out the sheet saying I did 100 hours of shadowing and then mail it to my teacher."

I usually felt fatigued. Nothing too serious, just a mild like light-headed sensation losing your breath after running up a flight of stairs. This time I felt nothing.

When I saw her face, I realized I wasn't afraid. The eyes and the smile were individually so menacing. But together, on her, they seemed . . . beckoning.

"Hold still," I said. She smiled the whole time. While

I stepped forward, smile. When I tilted her chin, smile. As our lips pressed together, SMILE.

It didn't last long. I only needed a moment to realize what I was doing. We separated. Then I felt it. The wind flew out from my lungs. "Forget this happened," I panted.

I dived for the exit. I had one foot out of her office when I stopped. "Tell your husband I enjoyed meeting him."

Her glassy stare followed me. It followed me through the walls of her office and held me captive as I attempted to pry open the front door.

***

When I was six, I beat my friend in a staring contest. "Now you have to kiss my butt, loser."

I felt violated when his teeth pierced my jeans.

That night Mom told me I was different from other kids. "You're just like an adult," she said. "Kids have to do what you tell them. You're special, but you've got to keep it secret." She told me if anyone ever discovered I was an "undercover adult," I would have to start reading the newspaper and couldn't go outside for recess.

During the next few months, I felt like a spy. I

watched my teachers from the corners of my eye. I wondered if they knew that I was secretly one of them. One time a girl in my class told me that teachers had eyes in the back of their head. I spent the night examining my skull in the bathroom mirror.

I watched what I said to other kids. However, Mom was an adult. Since she was a grown up like me, I reasoned it was alright to talk back to her.

"I don't want salad," I said.

"It's what I made," she said. Even at that age, I knew she was tired. She had to fill in the extra shifts at her store.

"Throw it out and make me cookies," I said. The change happened instantly. Her tired eyes became glassy and dilated.

She smiled. *God, I still remember it.* "How many would you like?"

"I'll tell you when to stop."

I intended to stop her, but after I ate the first batch I fell asleep on the couch watching cartoons. When I woke up around midnight, the house had the distinct warm smell of the local bakery, only burning. The kitchen was stacked with more piles of cookies than I could count, much less eat. We must have run out of cookie dough because the blender and mixing bowl were out. The oven was emitting smoke from all sides.

Then I saw her. Mom came trotting into the kitchen smiling with a new bag of flour. She didn't even look at me. Her eyes were only fixed on the mixing bowl. *Oh those eyes.*

"Mom, you can stop now."

The smile disappeared, and Mom collapsed to the floor. The flower bag hit the ground and the top part erupted, leaving a white stain in the center of Mom's work shirt. I noticed her feet were trailing blood. When I told someone to do something, they always acted happy about it, like it was their idea. It was the first time I saw Mom cry since Dad left.

Mom told me the truth after that. "You're special baby." Her fingers parted my hair as she spoke. "When you talk, everyone no matter who they are will listen. Everyone will listen and everyone will obey."

I stayed awake all night. I wondered, if I wasn't an adult, then, what was I?

***

A month after Charlie transferred schools, I gave up on being a surgeon or any kind of hero. I majored in Biology to keep Mom happy, but complemented it with minors in business and communications.

I still used my powers in college, but to a lesser degree: an extended assignment here, a make-up test there . . . I tried not to use my abilities at all, but I wasn't capable. Physically, I couldn't do it. A week without commanding a single person left me drained. I barely had the strength to get out of bed. *I was screwed either way*. Not controlling people took more out of me than controlling them. I **needed** to use my powers, I **needed** the adrenaline. It was like an addiction. Only it was different than a pill or liquor bottle, it was a part of me.

Sometimes I wished my abilities away. I did when Charlie transferred. However, these moments were scarce. The thought of not having my powers scared me more than the powers themselves. Without them, I'd be so vulnerable.

I mostly kept to myself in college, but I didn't keep myself in complete isolation. I joined a couple clubs and even went to a few parties. Though I didn't drink. One time freshman year, I got drunk and told a senior who was a TA in my class to give me a blow job in the bathroom. I suppose it was fortunate I came to my senses before anything serious happened. While we didn't *make love*, we did have an enlightening conversation about her dream of being a teacher. "It's sooooo funny," she slurred. "They actually pay you to tell children what to do. Pay's shit, but it's pay." Working with children started to sound intriguing.

I didn't want the up close and personal nature of a public school, so I researched jobs at local learning centers. They were places where kids were tutored on an individual basis. Certified teachers worked with the kids, while a manager ran the company, and an administrator worked with the clients and teachers. The administrator job seemed perfect for me. The only people I'd have to deal with in person were misbehaving children. Most adult conversations took place over the phone. My "gift" only worked if I talked to someone face to face.

Mom wasn't as thrilled with my selection. "Are you going to waste your life being some small town administrator?"

I told her it was what I wanted.

"Anyone can teach," she said. "Surgeons, political leaders . . . They save lives. Baby, you can change the world."

Hearing those words made me furious. "What the fuck does a grocery store owner know about the world!"

She seized my arm. "Glenn, you need to listen to me," she screamed even though she was only inches from my face.

I smiled. "Actually mother, aren't you the one who **needs** to listen to me?"

Her fingers trembled as she released me. She took a step back. The further she moved from me, the more her eyes widened to make up the difference. "Glenn," she said. I wasn't letting her win, not this time. I just kept staring her down.

Following our conversation, I started looking for job openings out of state.

About a month after I moved, I got an interview. It

was a privately owned tutoring center in a small city. They were looking for an assistant manager. The manager was a young blonde woman named Megan. She looked like one of my elementary school teachers. Her round face and soft eyes made her attractive, but in a motherly way.

It wasn't hard to convince her to give me a job. I didn't need my powers. I spent my whole life talking to people like teachers talk to children. "The important thing to remember is that kids are very impressionable," I said. "It's important to choose your words carefully. The same is true with parents and teachers. It would be my job to work with them and guide them, not to tell them what to do."

Her smile didn't bother me like Mrs. Hatcher's did. Where Mrs. Hatcher's was a planted toothy grin, Megan only used her lips, but it was genuine and twice as effective. "We're a small business," she said. "You would have to teach some kids on busy days. Would that be a problem?"

"Not at all. My Mom used to tell me I was like an undercover teacher. This doesn't seem much different."

She had a quiet laugh.

The administrator job worked out well. I'm a fairly

organized person. My co-workers were alright. I had no trouble taking calls from parents and telling teachers over the phone when to be at work. However, the biggest perk was the children. *Oh those wonderful misbehaving brats.*

The kids really made the job feel like a spy movie. They threw tantrums, spit balls, and anything else they could get their spastic fingers on. Like clockwork, the teachers approached my desk, suspects in hand. "Jenny and Mary are going to stay in time out until one of them confesses to throwing the calculator at Matt."

I had my mission. "No need," I looked into both their wondering eyes. "Jenny, Mary . . . You both are going to show me who threw the calculator." *Interrogation initiated.* Their raised hands reflected in their glassy eyes. Both fingers pointed to Jenny. *Culprit acquired.* "Thank you. Jenny, apologize to Matt. Then both of you get back to work."

Megan asked me to stay behind and help her close the center after one particularly busy day. "You did a good job today," she said as she locked her office door. "Reilly really listened to you. I've never been able to get him to work so hard. And he wasn't sulking either."

"It was nothing."

"I disagree." She took a moment and stared out the window into the dark sky. The moon was full that night. She closed her eyes and inhaled. She seemed captivated by its glow. "My father didn't think I should try to manage a company. I know this business isn't much, but he said even then people weren't going to take me seriously."

I didn't have a father to compare with, but it sounded like bad parenting. "If you want, I'll call him and personally vouch for the great job you're doing."

She bit her lip for a moment before she spoke. "Glenn, would you like to grab dinner?"

Megan and I went to dinner three times and the bar twice before she invited me back to her place. She lived on the top floor of an upscale apartment complex. It seemed just a little more than a small town employee could afford, but that was the best way to define Megan. Always a little more.

We spent most of the evening on her balcony. She

insisted we take advantage of the moon light. I asked why we needed to freeze our asses off when there was a fireplace inside. I was always careful to **ask** with Megan.

"Shoot for the moon. Even if you miss, you'll land among the stars." She whispered the words as if she were in the habit of saying them to herself. I knew she was quoting Norman Vincent Peale, but in my mind it was her own fountain of wisdom.

I remembered the full moon growing up. Mom would take me outside. Together we would sit on our porch and admire its beauty. She said I was like the moon and she said I was like the moon, while normal people were the stars. "Sometimes you're covered by darkness, but when you glow you're brighter than anyone."

In a lot of ways, Megan was like my mother. In many more ways, she was something else entirely. Her presence grounded me. Perhaps the way her eyebrows lifted when she was excited, or the way her head seemed to nod in rhythm to my words.

We slept together that night. It was her first time with me and my first time with anyone. It was amazing. I felt everything about her. *Her touch, smell, taste.* But the best part was her smile. The completely genuine grin of hers. She took it to bed and I wore it the next morning. It faded after I walked into her kitchen and saw the morning news.

The anchors were reporting a missing child. I missed the name, but the caption indicated he was in the 7th grade. When they showed his picture, I felt something slither inside my chest. A lot of young boys look alike, but this kid looked just like Charlie.

"That's a shame," Megan said. "We waste so much time reporting cat videos and local sales, meanwhile who's looking for this kid?" I think she continued to speak, but I stopped listening.

***

It was long ago, but the image felt burned in my brain. The hair was different. Charlie had darker hair and a sharper, more pressed together face, but I think that came with age. Other than that, the resemblance was astounding.

Charlie was in the 9th grade when he went missing. My high school called everyone to a meeting in the auditorium and passed around fliers with his basic

information: hair color- brown, eye color- blue, height- 5'6
. . .

I was a junior at the time. Like any boy my age, I entertained the fantasy of being a secret agent. For me, the dream could be reality. I imagined myself traveling to foreign countries, escorted by at least 6 secret service men, where I would lead terrorist interrogations. Maybe I would grow a beard? That part was debatable. Otherwise, I had the whole thing planned out. I wouldn't immediately make them tell me the information we needed. It needed to be believable. Still, I'd get results. I'd find hidden bombs, uncover deadly spies, and save countless lives.

I remember being more excited than troubled by Charlie's disappearance. It was the perfect opportunity for spy training. In first period I barely listened to Mr. Howard's wig rant. Why did I need to? I'd be exempt from all classwork once I found the missing freshman. I could see the newspapers: **Charlie's Angel Comes to Town to Save the Life of Local 9th Grader.**

I took lunch period to contemplate my strategy. At first, I thought I would make his parents tell me where they last saw him. But I didn't want to involve them unless absolutely necessary. Besides, asking his friends might prove more beneficial. It's possible they knew more than they let on, but that strategy was flawed. I didn't know his friends. I couldn't even remember seeing his face from across the hallway between classes. I finally decided to start with the neighborhood.

I spent hours questioning Charlie's neighbors. It took much longer than I anticipated. Something didn't feel right about knocking on someone's door and immediately making them tell me everything they knew about a missing child. I always introduced myself and explained my mission. Many invited me inside.

"Aren't you such a brave, kind young man? Would you like some cookies?" a large woman, three doors down from Charlie's house, said. Her eyes became misty when I asked her to tell me what she knew about Charlie. She managed to sigh through her smile. It was honestly quite disturbing. I could tell she was sad, but she still had that damn smile.

"Oh, it's so tragic. I believe I saw him last week by

the pond. He looked like he was playing some game with a larger boy. Then again, they might have been fishing."

The problem with making people telling you the truth was that it was always their version of the truth. Some neighbors thought they saw him fishing while others thought he was at the market. Some even insisted that government officials took him, to draw attention away from how they were polluting our waters.

It was a quarter past nine when I reached Charlie's house. Mom knew I would be out late, but I hadn't eaten dinner or started any of my homework. I already felt weak from commanding the twenty-some neighbors. I looked up towards the sky. The stars and most of the moon were smothered in fog.

Charlie's parents lived in a two-story house in a nice neighborhood, but their house was different from the others. It was as if an extra shade of darkness had crept across the yard and shrouded the entire building. The only visible light came from a dimly lit lamp in the bottom window, behind the closed curtain.

I slowly approached the looming house. I paused at

the mailbox. Their family name was printed in bold letters. I read each one slowly- A L D R I C H. I read them forwards, backwards, and any other way possible. Anything to avoid entering that house. *What was I going to say? How was I going to say it?* My stomach twitched. I made it halfway down the driveway and then went home.

The next day I felt weak. Not the slight weakness I got after using my powers. This was a draining feeling I'd never experienced before. I could barely lift my head to see I'd overslept. *Fuck Charlie. Fuck his damn family.*

Mom called the school and said I was sick. As the day progressed, I began to feel trapped. Being alone with my thoughts was almost as bad as being in school. Mom worked late, so I had some time. I met some friends when school let out and told them to see a movie with me.

Unfortunately, a superhero movie was playing. The last thing I wanted to see was stoic man with veins bulging from his biceps attempt to save the world. I watched the meat-head get beaten time after time. Yet, he still managed to rescue his super-model girlfriend.

I envied how my friends were able to eat their popcorn and grin wide-eyed into the theater screen. They didn't think twice about Charlie because, besides flipping through a couple of bent fliers, there was nothing they could do.

I saw Charlie the next day. His picture was on the news while Mom and I were eating breakfast. It was one of him smiling while holding a large fish on a hook. His parents came on the screen next. The father spoke while the mother gazed longingly into the screen. She wore a turtleneck sweater and pearl earrings. Her glassy stare made me think she was looking at me.

"Charlie loves the outdoors. He always wants to be close to a lake or pond." He said. "Please help us find our son. He needs to come home." He was balding slightly, and she was just a touch overweight.

Following Charlie's announcement, a story about two masked men robbing a local bank filled the screen. In the movies there was always just one criminal or one missing child, and the hero always figured out what to do.

"Doesn't he go to your school?" Mom asked. "Did you know him?"

"No," I said. I grabbed my book bag and left for class. She didn't need words to let me know she was disappointed.

A L D R I C H. I read the letters twice before walking down the driveway.

Charlie's mother was sitting on the front porch. I recognized her from the television. This time she was wearing sweat pants and a t-shirt. I wondered what she was really like. I didn't spend any time getting to know her. "You need to stay here and answer all my questions," I said before I even reached the porch steps.

Her smile made my stomach turn. I sat next to her on one of the wooden chairs and tried to avoid her eyes. She held a cigarette between her fingers. The smoke spiraled off the charred end. She tapped it against her chair's arm and let the burned tip fall to the floor. That was probably the closest I would get to knowing the true Mrs. Aldrich. A woman with a fake smile, flicking away dead cigarette butts.

"Do you think your son was kidnapped?"

"He wasn't kidnapped," she said. "He ran away. His fishing bag's missing. He must've filled it with supplies."

"Tell me if you have any idea where he went."

"I know where he went," she exhaled some smoke and coughed on the vapor. "He's at the clubhouse."

"Did you see him there? Tell me everything you know."

"I didn't see him." She lowered her cigarette and leaned close to me. Her breath smelled like tar. "I know that boy better than anyone on this earth. He's at the clubhouse. It's an abandoned shack in the woods. We used to go fishing there when he was younger."

A true detective investigates every angle. I didn't. Once she told me where to find the clubhouse, I was satisfied. I didn't ask any more questions, not even obvious ones like *Why didn't you tell the police about the clubhouse?* or *What made him run away?*

The one thing I'm proud of is staying with her while she finished the cigarette. We didn't speak except for when

I left and told her to forget our conversation. It was the only instance where I actually did something for the Aldrich family. During that time, we sat under the moonlight while the smoke currents swirled around my head.

The shack hardly resembled a club house. It was constructed with 100-year-old wood that had to be termite infested. Mosquitoes and crab grass surrounded it on all sides. The front door felt as though it would crumble to bits in my hand, and once I pushed it open the smell nearly toppled me. The inside reeked of shit and rotten fish. It didn't seem a hospitable environment for any living creature.

But there was life. A boy; brown hair, blue eyes. He shrieked when he saw me.

"Don't be afraid of me." I whispered those words. I whispered everything to him. I don't know why.

I studied him for a moment. He looked like the picture on the news, minus the fish and plus some dirt. "Tell me your name," I said.

He uttered the only words I ever heard him say,

"Charlie Aldrich." His voice was different than expected. It was deep sounding for a boy who just spent three days playing Hide and Go Seek in the woods.

His glassy eyes followed me to his house. He carried with him a backpack filled with two bottles of water, three apples, a half-eaten box of Oreos, a change of clothes, fifty-four dollars and thirty-eight cents, a fishing rod with bait, and a baseball bat.

As we walked, I continued to look back to make sure he was still following. He kept his head down while he moved through the twigs and leaves. I liked it that way. I couldn't see his smile.

We stopped at his mailbox. "Read each letter frontwards and backwards to yourself ten times," I said. "After you finish, you will go inside your house and forget that you saw me." I turned his head and looked directly into his lifeless eyes. "You will never run away from home again."

The full moon was bright. It allowed me to keep an eye on Charlie once I was a few streets away. Its light shined on him as Charlie walked down his driveway. I really was the moon. The stars all tried, but *I illuminated the path for Charlie*. And I glowed.

Following Charlie's return, I felt invincible. No one fully knew how or why he returned. When asked, he said he didn't remember much of the night. People were calling it a miracle.

I ordered people to do my bidding. Students carried my books, teachers bought me lunch, quiet girls cussed out teachers, valedictorians mooned principals, doctor's wives made out with me . . . *They owed it to me.*

For the first and only time in my life, I watched with pride as my words turned people into shells. The adrenaline swam through my veins as dilated eyes danced for my amusement. *I never felt more alive . . .*

Two months before I graduated, Charlie's father was arrested. I don't know the reason, and I hope to never know.

Some say they saw Charlie hiding bruises. Others say Mr. Aldrich sold pictures of Charlie pleasuring himself. The ones I really wanted to punch said Charlie had a funny walk,

"Like someone's been shoving a stick up his ass for years."

A month before the arrest and Charlie being sent to Foster Care and forced to transfer schools, Mrs. Aldrich left. Though people were divided about Mr. Aldrich, they all felt the same about her. "What kind of mother would run away and leave her child with a monster?" They said. For all I know, she tried to take him with her.

Often, I repeat my last words to Charlie. "You will never run away from home again."

***

"Oh, someone's in trouble." A teacher said when Megan called me into her office. My co-workers loved to tease me about dating my boss. To them, she controlled me in the work place and in bed. *Little did they know . . .*

I was careful to never use my abilities on Megan, but the fact that I could was somewhat thrilling. On the outside she was in command, and I let her be. She picked the restaurants, she set the work schedule, she chose when to call me into her office and slip her hand down my pants . . . But underneath it all, unbeknown to even Megan, I was in command. *It was my secret pleasure.*

Megan shut the door and closed the blinds, the way she always did. Though something was off. Normally, she was quick to conceal our moments and even quicker to get started. This time she moved slowly and didn't initiate contact. When she finished, she walked behind her desk. It was like a barrier between us.

"I just got off the phone with your mother," she said. The erection I had been trying to hide, fell flaccid. The only thing I didn't like about Megan was how she threw Mom in my face. I hadn't seen my mother in over a year. The last time we talked was on her birthday. I made the mistake of using Megan's phone to call. Since then, they've talked every week.

She always told me, every time they spoke. "Your mother's so sweet," she would say. "She needs to come for a visit one of these days." Megan was like a window between Mom's world and mine. She knew it, and she liked it. She bragged about using new dinner recipes that Mom taught her and caught me up on the latest gossip at Mom's store. A few months ago she signed up for a YOGA class. "**Your Mom** convinced me," she said. "Did you know she does YOGA three times a week?" She never mentioned one word about her own mother, maybe that's why she was so obsessed with mine.

"Your mother wants to see you," she said.

"*Really*? She asked for me? Well, I feel honored."

"This is serious," Megan said. She bit her lip just like the night she asked me out. "There's something else. She wanted me to tell you . . . she . . . she has cancer."

I don't know what I said. *Perhaps I didn't respond.* I must've taken a seat, because the next thing I knew Megan was in my lap. "It'll be alright," she said. She parted my hair the way I liked, and pressed her warm lips to my forehead.

Strangely, I wasn't thinking about my mother. In that moment, the only thoughts that came to mind were of Charlie. I wondered what became of him.

Megan and I were quiet for most of the drive. I was happy she came with me, but I wasn't in the mood to talk. The house seemed smaller than I remembered. Even under the dim moonlight, the front porch didn't look sturdy enough to hold a mother and child as they rocked under the stars.

I barely recognized Mom when she opened the door. She was never an overly attractive lady, but I didn't have words to describe the sickly bag of wrinkles that stood before me. She held herself open for a hug. The ridged edge of her spine stuck to my arms as they folded around her. She must have lost over fifty pounds.

I didn't know if I wanted to keep holding her or kill her myself. "How are you feeling, Mom?"

"Oh, I'm fine," she tried to hide the slight gargle in her voice. "You guys must be exhausted. Come inside, I made some food."

At dinner Mom and Megan danced around any mention of health. Instead they talked about the grocery store and the increasing cost of air travel. "I know," Mom said. "I saw on the news that you can't get a flight out of the country for less than $1000. It's unreal." *She had never even been out of the state.*

"Is there somewhere you really want to go?" Megan asked. I wanted to vomit at her look of genuine interest. It was as if every word Mom spat out was laced in gold.

"Oh, I don't know." Mom paused to put the tiniest bit of a broken cookie in her mouth. "There're so many things to consider . . . cost, weather . . ."

"Well, you better make up your mind fast. Isn't time running out?"

"Glenn!" Megan gave me her best angry whisper.

"It's alright sweetie," I said. "Go sit in the other room. I'll join you in a minute." That was the first time I ever used my abilities on Megan. That smile, *that awful grin*. It was like an icepick in my chest. *Now I was mad*.

Once Megan was out of earshot, I stood up and glared at the bag of bones. "You couldn't tell me **yourself** that you have cancer? Were you too busy swapping recipes with Megan to give me a call?"

For a moment she stood still. "Last time I told you something you didn't want to hear, you moved away." It looked as if she needed to focus all her energy to contract her lips. "I'm not like you, Glenn. People don't always **have to** accept what I tell them."

There it was. "You think my ability is so amazing, don't you? Do you have any idea what is was like, growing up having to watch every word I said? I didn't ask for these fucking powers, but they're part of me. I can't ignore them."

"But you don't need to suppress your abilities. People everywhere have talents they were born with to make the world a better place."

"So, you want me to use my powers? You punished me for it!"

"When you were taking advantage of people, but think about what you could do. With one word, you could stop a war and save millions of lives. Instead you waste your talents on childish antics, trying to be . . ."

"Be what Mom?" I said. "**Normal**?"

She froze. Her stare was unknown, yet so familiar. She looked cold, but underneath it there was fear. I recognized it now, just like I failed to recognize it in the eyes of Charlie's mother. I *needed* to know what she was thinking.

"Tell me the truth, Mom." Her eyes changed. Now, they had nothing behind them. Below those glassy eyes, it had returned. The smile I had avoided for so long. The one whose blood-stained foot prints crept through the darkest corners of my mind. I could almost smell the cookies burning in the oven.

If she was making me go through this, I was getting some damn answers. "Are you ashamed of me?"

I waited through the longest seconds I ever experienced. Mom seemed to move her lips in slow motion. "You should be ashamed of me. I'm the one who is too fat, old, and ugly."

I heard Mom say those words before, but this was the first time I knew what they meant. She wasn't ashamed of my powers, she was jealous. With them, she could've stopped what she lost.

"Mom, stop blaming yourself for Dad. For the rest of your life remember that he didn't leave because of you. He's just a rotten bastard."

The smile nodded, then I told her to forget our conversation.

I don't know if I made the right decision. I was never able to use my abilities on myself. I didn't know if it was better to feel fake happiness or true sadness. What I do know is that I never saw my mother smile more than she did during the last three months of her life. It wasn't the smile I forced on her, it was genuine.

The human mind is so complex, and yet so malleable by my words. Still, something as simple as a microscopic cancerous cell is above and beyond my abilities. They didn't change a thing when it came to my mother's fate.

She couldn't speak when she died, but I was able to hold her hand and stare into her eyes. Ironically, they looked warm and full of life, much more so than anyone else I ever commanded.

I often think back to the night my mother died. It was in the forefront of my mind the day I walked into the social services office and told them I wanted a job in the child protection department.

Usually, her death is not what I remember. I think about after, when I joined Megan on one of the lumpy waiting room couches. The two of us stared out the window into the pale light of the full moon. I don't know how much time passed before I spoke.

"Do you think she was proud of me?"

"She told me you were going to change the world."

I had to shut my eyes because they filled with tears. I felt Megan's arms wrap around my body and press me to hers. I think that was when I knew I could tell her the truth about me.

When I finally opened my eyes, the moon seemed just a little brighter. It was the light in a dark abyss filled with fading stars that stretched over a universe of endless possibilities. But at that moment, I glowed the strongest as I remained locked in place by Megan's arms.

The Perfect House

Kathrine sat erect on the couch in her living room. Frustrated, she placed her computer on the coffee table and held two fingers before her lips as she often did while in deep thought. The only text on her open word document was the title "The Perfect House." She took a moment to reflect on how the title so clearly echoed her residence. The couch was unstained despite years of use, with pillows fluffed and strategically placed. The coffee table supporting her laptop remained dustless, sitting atop a rug exactly centered on the floor with each of its end tassels intact.

The woman was in her mid-forties, though from observing how tidy she kept herself and the upright manner in which she walked, the average person would suspect she was in her thirties. She retreated to the kitchen and poured a glass of wine. Kathrine removed the knife from its holder and sliced a single piece of lemon. She made sure to wash the knife and clean the countertop before placing the slice on the rim of her spotless glass.

Returning to her computer, Kathrine sipped the wine and mulled over the words of her publisher. "Write what you know," he had said while puffing a cigar, causing Kathrine to keep a sizable distance. "You got me swimin' in a sea of beautiful language, but ya dialogue's shit." At that point he had held up Kathrine's manuscript and slammed it on his desk. "Your girl's words are too crisp and proper sounding, nobody talks like that."

Though Kathrine never admitted it aloud, she agreed with the critique. She disliked conversations and tended to avoid them when possible. As a child she kept to herself, electing to spend her lunch periods reading rather than socializing. Now an adult, she lived on the Appalachian Mountains, near the peak of a smaller mount. For Kathrine, the location was ideal.

Her cabin provided a secure three miles of separation between her and the nearest community. The house didn't contain phone lines, the writer preferred the smooth sound of water trickling through mountain rocks to the uneven and often disruptive sounds of other people, so the device seemed useless. However, the isolation had taken its toll. She'd forgotten many fundamentals of maintaining conversations; how to introduce oneself, the appropriate length of pause between sentences, the correct volume level to exhibit . . .

As Kathrine glanced at the unfinished project, she noticed the computer had faded to black. She reached to reopen the device when something in the darkened screen caught her eye. A figure, expanding steadily in size. A chill seeped into Kathrine's chest as she realized it was a person.

She ducked, narrowly missing the slash of the man's blade. She felt the wind inches above her neck. In these moments, Kathrine's body reacted differently from others. Her pulse remained the same, but her mind accelerated. She smashed the wine glass against the coffee table and stabbed the intruder's chest with the jagged edge.

"Bitch!" The man screamed amidst his howls of pain. Kathrine raced for the staircase. There was no one for miles and her car keys were in the basement, upstairs was her best option. Halfway up, she heard the man scramble to his feet.

Kathrine dived into her bedroom, locked the door, and dashed into her closet. She had just enough time to notice her hand was dripping with blood. The glass must have cut her too. Savage beating erupted from the bedroom door. She clenched her bloody hand when she heard the lock break.

"Bitch . . ." He said slowly, his voice almost mocking. "Where are you?" Kathrine heard his fingers drag against the wall. She heard her bed sheets ruffle. He was checking under the bed. "Think you can hide?" His tone still mocking. Now he was standing, facing the closet. Although Kathrine couldn't see the intruder, she felt his eyes glaring through the door at her. She envisioned the smile stretching across his face. The sadistic grin of the mountain lion as she corners her prey.

"I'm going to twist this knife right up your cunt," his

voice a chilling mixture of mockery and rage. With every word, the voice drew closer. She closed her eyes and blocked out the sound of her steady heartbeat. She listened. The sound of the intruder's jagged breath drew closer. She waited, knowing he was taking his time. One of them would have to make a move.

The doorknob twitched. Kathrine lunged forward, slamming the door forward into the man's face. The man fell. He wailed, slashing his blade through the air. Kathrine sprang from the closet just before he kicked the door shut.

Without looking back, she ran to the staircase. She darted down, taking the steps three at a time. She tripped on the last step, catching herself before hitting the ground. Feeling him on her feet, she jumped to the left, just missing his grasp.

She ran into the kitchen and pressed herself into the corner cabinets. With nowhere to run, she turned to confront the intruder. He walked slowly into the kitchen doorframe, his rusty blade clenched tightly between his fingers. Blood was lingering on his chest. His face was unshaven and narrow, as if pointing towards her. He licked his lips twice. Kathrine stared into the man's eyes for the first time. They were blistered with rage.

He charged at her. The sound of metal piercing flesh echoed through the ceiling tiles. The intruder fell to the ground. He didn't see her pull the kitchen knife.

***

Two hours later, Kathrine's house was consistent with its usual standards; the pillows were fluffed, the rug was aligned, and the stains (both wine and blood) were removed. The home's owner stood on its front porch, holding two fingers before her lips in the manner one would hold a cigarette. She inhaled deeply and exhaled slowly, her lips forming an oval shape.

She couldn't deny or repress what had happened. Tonight, she almost died. Kathrine drew another breath, taking in the fresh scent of the mountain air. Feeling the crisp wind flow freely in her lungs helped return her to a cool and collective state. Steadily, she reentered the cabin, latching the door behind her.

The writer passed her computer. Though some would find it atypical, the thought of her story crept to mind. Briefly, the seed was planted for her to use the night's events to her advantage. A horror story; a mountain killer, a confrontation, a struggle between life and death . . . Inspiration had come from an unlikely outlet.

Kathrine approached the steps to her basement. Cautiously, she descended the dimly-lit staircase. Her foot made contact with the concrete pavement and she proceeded across the floor. When she reached the freezer, the woman paused briefly before opening it. The bitter air rushed against Kathrine's unflinching face.

She placed the intruder's severed head next the heads of his wife and two children. "Write what you know," she said in a voice far too soft and slow for regular conversation. She adjusted the man's head so it was in line with the others. A smile contorted across her face, before the perfect, even row.

Forgotten Letters of the Dead

There was a city fair the night Kyle learned of Jake and Tammy. The numerous lights had alternated red and orange to honor the Halloween season. The event housed a Ferris Wheel, three haunted houses, and most importantly a 300-foot-tall rollercoaster, The Midnight Madness.

Kyle joined his friends' table with a warm funnel cake. The white frosting was designed to look like spiderwebs. "You guys want some of this?"

"I'll pass." Tammy said.

"Come on Tammy. You know you want a bite."

"I said no." She looked around. "Do you guys want to go on the hay ride? The line looks short."

"You don't go to a Halloween fair for a hay ride. It's all about the roller coasters and haunted houses."

"Well, I don't do roller coasters and I don't like being scared."

"We'd protect you." Kyle flexed his arm. "Right Jake?"

"I wouldn't trust either of you." She moved behind Kyle and ruffled the mop of hair on his head. "Well, I'm going on the hay ride. Are you coming Jake?"

"A coaster does sound fun." Jake said.

She scrunched her face. "Suit yourself."

After Tammy was out of earshot, Jake turned to Kyle. He was midway through stuffing a handful of funnel cake down his throat. The frosting smeared the corner of his lips. "You're not going to tell her?"

Kyle took a moment to chew. "Not tonight." He wiped his mouth with his sleeve.

"Are you sure you're alright?"

"Yeah . . . I guess. I didn't really know him."

"When did you last see him?"

"Nine years, maybe ten." Kyle took another bite.

"Nine." He nodded. "It was close to Halloween when he left. Mom didn't take me trick or treating that year. I was six then, so nine. A kid doesn't forget missing trick or treating. It's traumatizing."

"You didn't see him at all?"

"Not in person. He called sometimes; my birthday, a Christmas here and there. He never said much. And if he even heard Mom's voice, he'd find some excuse to hang up."

"I'm sorry."

"You're not the one who abandoned your family, twice." He chuckled. "If you count heart failure as abandonment."

"Still sucks."

"Well there is actually one up side. He left me something pretty cool." Jake raised an eyebrow. "I'll tell you if you can brave the Midnight Madness with me."

The line to the ticket station was long. It gave Kyle

and Jake ample time to identify all the screamers. The guy in the sweater-vest, "Total screamer." The bald man with bicep tattoos, "High-pitched squealer." Girl with the pink hair bow, "Silent warrior."

When they neared the end of the line, Kyle and Jake observed the couple in front of them. They appeared to be in their mid-twenties. The girl was pressed against the guy's side. She had his arm encased in hers. She appeared to be moving her feet to the tune of some Irish jig. That, or she was just cold.

"I bet the girl is a screamer." Jake whispered in Kyle's ear.

"Are you thinking scary movie gasp or Tammy level shriek?" Kyle whispered back.

The couple approached the ticket man. "Six dollars please," the ticket man said. A quick cash exchange and the couple ushered into the coaster's loading platform.

Kyle and Jake approached the ticket station.

"Three dollars please."

"Oh, we're paying together," Kyle said.

"Ahh," The ticket man smiled. "I shouldn't have

assumed. That'll be six dollars."

Kyle handed the man a couple of crumpled up bills, then led Jake inside.

The loading platform stretched out before them. Kyle watched the Midnight Madness creep up the track with its next victims. The worn wooden track looked ricketier up close. It was perfect! Even better, the line for the front seat was open. He and Jake quickly filled the spot.

"That guy was weird." Jake said.

"The ticket taker? I know. He wanted us to pay . . . With money. What a freak." Kyle laughed.

Jake rolled his eyes. "Why'd he say he shouldn't assume?"

"Cause he almost charged us the wrong amount?"

"But why'd he smile?"

"Who cares?" Kyle shook his head. "It almost seems like you're trying to delay the ride, Tammy."

Jake didn't respond. The Midnight Madness had completed its cycle and was pulling into the loading dock. Mixed expressions of adrenalin, exhaustion, and confusion encircled the riders as they staggered off the coaster.

"These things are so freeing," Kyle said once they were seated.

"You call being strapped to a ten-ton machine freeing?"

"Not like that. When you're racing down that first drop, the adrenaline takes over. You can say whatever you want; it's pure instinct. And no one will know what your instincts make you say." He tuned to Jake and half shrugged. "They'll just hear your screams."

As the Midnight Madness started its jerky ascent, Kyle's grip on the handlebar tightened. He wondered if his father liked roller coasters as much as he did. His mom didn't, so he had to get it from somewhere.

As the coaster reached its peak, Kyle tried to recall if he'd ever mentioned roller coasters to his dad. He couldn't remember. In fact, he couldn't remember much of anything they ever discussed.

Kyle stared at Jake as the Midnight Madness dove towards the earth. His head was bent down, against the wind. His mouth was moving. Perhaps a scream? Perhaps a secret?

There were several things Kyle thought about saying. But instinct took control and paved a different path. His words dissolved in the night air, abandoned as he raced further down the track. "Why did you leave?"

***

Kyle walked the six flights of stairs to his apartment. He avoided the elevator whenever possible. He didn't have anything against elevators but enjoyed the exercise and time to think the steps provided. He needed them both today.

Tammy wouldn't be caught dead walking up the stairs. The thought made him laugh, then scowl. She thought she had the big news to share. She had a boyfriend now! Great for her. She had pulled him to the side after the Midnight Madness to share the wonderful news. Kyle let her have her time in the spotlight. For her curtain call he added, "My dad died today."

It wasn't technically true. His dad died three days ago, but the executor hadn't contacted Kyle or his mother until today. Saying "today" just gave the statement more of a punch. Kyle wished he had taken a picture of Tammy's face. Her confidence flushed in a matter of seconds. Jake just looked terrified the entire time. And Tammy thought she was the one that scared easily.

Kyle reached the door to his apartment. Once inside, the first thing he noticed was the pile in the kitchen sink. That didn't make sense. It had been emptied in the morning. Upon closer inspection, he saw it was filled with beer bottles.

His mother's work bag was on the kitchen table. It was turned sideways with its contents spilled. Papers were scattered across the table and the surrounding floor. He called for his mom, but she didn't answer. He tried her cell phone, but it went to voicemail.

Kyle's mother entered the apartment well after midnight. She dropped her keys upon entry and nearly fell to the floor attempting to retrieve them. She took notice of her son sitting at the kitchen table.

"Did you wait up for me?" She gave a lazy smile. "That's so sweet."

"It's a school night, Mom." Kyle sighed.

"What? I don't get to go out? You went to the fair. It's only fair." She laughed. "Fair is fair!" She laughed harder.

"You should have some water, Mom." He gestured to the now empty kitchen sink.

The woman cocked her head. "Your father didn't like it when I went out, either. He'd tell me I needed to be more responsible." She hiccupped, then chuckled. "You think anyone would call him the responsible one now!"

She stopped laughed and abruptly walked into her bedroom. Kyle started to stand to follow her, but she quickly returned. She carried with her a rectangular brass box. She slammed it on the table and sat down next to Kyle.

She placed both her hands on the lid of the box. "You know what pisses me off the most about your father?"

She paused a moment. Kyle said nothing.

"Now that he's gone, he'll never see what I did. That I wasn't a complete fuck up." She placed both her hands on Kyle's cheeks and steered him to face her. "He'll never see what a beautiful boy you turned out to be."

***

Jake and Tammy sat at a small table in a local coffee shop. As was their custom, they seated themselves near the back corner.

"You sure this is a good idea?" Jake asked.

"Kyle loves this place." Tammy said. "Besides, he needs someone to talk to about his dad." She nodded in response to her statement.

"Won't it be a little awkward?"

"It's only awkward if we stop including Kyle." She placed her hand on Jake's and rubbed her thumb over his knuckles.

"Hey there, love birds." Kyle approached the table with his eyes locked on the phone in his hand. He squeezed a chair between Jake and Tammy and plopped down.

"Hey!" Tammy said. "We ordered you a hot chocolate."

Without meeting her eyes, Kyle took the cup. He never cared for the taste of coffee, but he loved the loved the aroma of ground beans that encased the humble shop. He tilted the Styrofoam container and let the warm liquid seep down his throat. Kyle exhaled deeply. His breath mounted inside the cup before pouring out and generating fog on his glasses.

They sat in silence for a while. Tammy briefly mentioned the approaching cold front and her plans for Thanksgiving. Jake contributed an, "oh nice," and a, "yeah."

Kyle was nearly finished with his drink when Tammy put her hand on his. "Do you want to talk about it?"

"About what?" Kyle continued to direct his gaze at the hot chocolate, so he didn't see Tammy flinch at his response. When she inhaled, Kyle spoke again. "I'm kidding . . . Yeah, we can talk, but not today. I need to get home. Mom will need me."

"How is she?" Jake asked.

"Fine." Standing up and adjusting his coat, Kyle took notice of the check perched on the table's end. He extended his arm.

"I got it." Jake held up the bill in one hand and fumbled in his pocket with the other.

"Please allow me." Kyle snatched the check from Jake's hand and stuffed a crisp bill into its fold. "I just had some money come in."

With that, he let the bill fall to the table. The resulting vibrations caused no more than a few ripples to expand in the couple's hot chocolates. Still, as the pair watched their friend leave, both bit their lips.

* * *

When Kyle entered the apartment, his mother was sitting at the kitchen table. Before her rested a familiar brass box adjacent to an empty bottle of beer.

She turned slowly to greet her son and forced a fragile smile. "How was school?"

"Fine . . . Lot of teachers asked when you'd be back."

She shook her head and laughed to herself. "You can't take two days off in that school without everybody losing their minds."

Kyle placed a ziplocked turkey sandwich next to the box. "You should have this."

His mom briefly eyed the meal. "I made this for your lunch."

"I know, but I ate out with Tammy and Jake." It was a lie, but Kyle suspected his mother had not made food for herself.

Occasionally, Kyle's mother required a push. When her husband left, the woman found herself unable to function. She couldn't work, eat, or even properly file for divorce.

The departure of Kyle's father seemed to leave a lingering scar on his mother. It was the kind that could be concealed but would never stop digging deeper. Perhaps the same was true for his father. The scar could have drilled down deep enough to finally stop his heart. The doctors provided no explanation more rational.

Kyle's mom was not very forthcoming with details regarding her husband. When Kyle spoke to his dad, he never asked him any real questions. He just usually responded to his father's usual comments: "How's school been treating you? "Is it still snowing, or has it started to warm up?" Kyle learned more about his father from the distribution of his estate than he ever had before.

His father had moved to Texas and worked as a guard in the Polunsky Unit. A quick google of the unit revealed it to be a large jail for holding male death row inmates. To even get clearance for such a job required years of training and experience. In addition, his father had nearly $100,000 in savings alone, which implied he was either a sharp money manager or rarely ventured from his home; possibly both.

"Did anything come in the mail?" Kyle asked.

Kyle's mother thumbed the hinges of the humble brass box. With her right index finger, the woman raised the lid before letting it fall. Click. The resulting sound was a high-pitched chime, mimicking the sound of two celebratory beer bottles being clinked together. She repeated the ritual three times before acknowledging her son's question. Click. Click. Click. "By the counter," she said.

When Kyle saw the envelope, he immediately knew what it contained. Since his parents were still technically married, he and his mother inherited everything. His mother had waived any right to her husband's more personal items. In general, Kyle had done the same, the one exception being the forgotten letters of the dead.

Forgotten letters of the dead was what Kyle called the hand-written notes found in his father's office. Kyle knew nothing about them, except that they referenced

Polunsky inmates. Due to the sensitivity of the subject matter, an investigation and censoring took place before Kyle could take custody. Kyle held the envelope before him, his hand nearly trembling.

Kyle's mom continued to examine the lid of her brass container. It had been years since that thing has seen the light of day, but now she wouldn't let it leave her side. Again, she opened the brass lid. She stared inside allowing her face to harden. His mother bit her bottom lip, then slammed the container shut. Click! She stood up and retreated to the refrigerator for another beer.

With those parting images, Kyle entered his bedroom and firmly planted himself at his desk chair. Kyle possessed many skills, but clean-cut letter opening was not included. He grasped the fold's end and slowly unstuck less than a fourth of an inch before the fold ripped, forcing him to repeat the procedure at the new end. The process was tedious and ugly but resulted in the successful opening of the first forgotten letter. Kyle took a moment to adjust his glasses, then began reading.

Dr. Mr. & Mrs. █████ *,*

I want to express my sorrow for your loss. No matter the circumstances, it is never easy to lose a child. I am one of the prison guards who was assigned to Trevor's cell. Over the years, we shared many conversations. In some ways, I considered him a friend.

Trevor talked about you two a lot. He recalled, fondly, memories of throwing ball in the back yard with his father. He knew you sometimes pretended to drop the ball in order to make him feel less embarrassed when he did the same. Mrs. █████ *, he said on more than one occasion that you were better than any five-star chef. Had the warden allowed it, he would have requested your apple pie as his last meal. My apologies if I am getting too personal.*

Over time, Trevor expressed remorse for what he did to that couple. He said it would have destroyed him had the same happened to you. In his final year, he found religion. He said prayers before he slept and spent hours each day studying the bible. Trevor was not a bad person, he simply lost control.

I sincerely hope this letter provides some peace of

mind. You two sound like wonderful parents. Please know your son loved you and hopes to see you again one day.

Yours Truly,

A Friend

***

Kyle sat erect at the desk adjacent to his bed, with the hand-written parcels separated before him. Jake stood a few feet away, craning his neck to skim the scattered documents. Tammy unwittingly assumed the buffer role, positioning herself between the two boys.

"It's impressive what your fath . . ." Jake trailed off. "What HE did."

"Apparently he got to know some of the inmates and wrote letters to their families after they died. I bet there are others." Kyle compiled and lifted the dead letters. "These must be the ones he never had time to send."

"What are you going to do with them?" Tammy asked.

"Read them!" Tammy and Jake both noticed a smile almost form on Kyle's face. "Then I guess I'll look into sending them. I mean this is too important for the families not to get them. The last names and addresses are blocked out, but it shouldn't be too hard to Google some recent executions."

"You're not keeping them?" Jake asked.

"I'd be a pretty selfish prick to do that, wouldn't I?"

Tammy placed her hand on the small of Kyle's back. She glided her fingers upward but didn't allow them to linger. She held herself partly responsible for Kyle's temper. She recognized Kyle's dismissive, and at times awkward, behavior as repressed feelings for her. She and Jake becoming an item constructed a degree of separation between them and Kyle. Furthermore, it diminished any hope Kyle had of ever being her boyfriend.

"What about your mom?"

Kyle spun around in his chair, facing Tammy and Jake for the first time since they entered his room. "What about her?"

"Has she read them?"

"She knows they exist."

"Don't you think it'd be nice . . ." Tammy said. "You know, for you to read them together."

Kyle suddenly snapped backward in his chair. The back was retractable, allowing him to nearly form a 180-degree angle. For a moment, his friends didn't know what to expect. Then he unleashed a bellowing, echoing laugh. "My God," he said between breaths. He sat up and locked eyes with Tammy. "You call subjecting someone to letters depicting graphic murder, written by a man who abandoned them, nice?" He continued to laugh.

Tammy gritted her teeth but concealed it with a smile she managed to form on her lips.

"While we're at it, what makes you think you know what my mom wants? Jake at least took one of her classes. Have you even said five words to her?"

Tammy nodded her head slowly. Then she abruptly snatched her backpack from Kyle's bed. "I'll see you tomorrow." She made her way towards the door. Once in the frame, she paused. Without looking back, she added "We're meeting at the coffee shop tomorrow. You're welcome to come." Then she made her exit.

"Aren't you going to go after her?" Kyle asked. "Isn't that what good boyfriends do?" He chuckled again.

"She's trying to help." Jake said sharply. Kyle waited for Jake to scamper out the door after Tammy, but he didn't move. "Do you want someone to read the letters with?" He said in a softer voice.

Kyle looked slightly started by the question. "And why would I want that?"

Jake avoided eye contact as he spoke. "You called us over here and haven't opened the others yet."

"So, you two are an 'us' now? I don't remember calling both of you." Kyle spun back around in his desk chair and resumed staring at the opened letter.

As Jake prepared to leave, he heard Kyle's voice. He didn't look away from the letters but spoke in a much softer tone. "I thought I'd open one a day. I'm not sure why, that just feels right."

Jake lowered his head, took a short breath, and proceeded across the room. "If you change your mind, I'm here for you." He placed his hand on Kyle's shoulder. Immediately, Kyle jerked away and spun around.

"Hey." Kyle waited for Jake to make eye contact. "Fuck you." He raised his middle finger and held it in place until Jake eventually left.

***

The next school day seemed to struggle on forever. Even classes that Kyle normally found amusing appeared to drag with a perpetual lull. It reminded Kyle of the old Peanuts cartoons, where all the adults would speak in incoherent monotones.

Finally, the dismissal bell rang. Kyle flung his backpack over his shoulder and set a course for home. He exited the classroom and made a bee-line down the hallway, rushing past the swarms of students who were just now existing their classes.

Just as the exit was in sight, Kyle felt a hand firmly clench his shoulder. Kyle winced fearing it may be Tammy; or worse Jake . . . Jake. A peculiar sensation overtook him. Like the eye of a tornado, Kyle slipped into a stationary calm amidst the surrounding chaos.

Kyle about faced, however he didn't find himself confronting Tammy or Jake. The plump figure that stood before him was his Geometry teacher.

"Hello there, Kyle," she said.

"Hey," he said quickly, trying not to look disappointed.

"Sorry to hold you up. I was just hoping you could tell me how your mother is doing."

"She's alright. She'll be back tomorrow."

"Oh." The woman's face briefly flinched. "Well . . . I was actually asked to cover her class for the rest of the week." Her pupils scampered to the corner of her eye as if recalling something. "Maybe I was misinformed. I'll double check." With that, she patted Kyle's shoulder, offered a few well-wishes, and waddled away.

***

When Kyle entered his apartment, his mother gasped. It was the kind of faint reflex that could only be heard by someone actively listening for it. She was still perched by the kitchen table, still sported her nightgown and beer bottle, and, of course, still had her hand planted on the lid of her brass box. She didn't greet Kyle; she only nodded quiet approval of his arrival.

Kyle nodded back and then proceeded past her. In the corner of his eye, he could see her thumbing the box's lid. She'd raise it slightly, then let it fall back into place. Click. His room was in sight. Click. He was almost there. Click. His hand was on the doorknob. Click. He paused. CLICK. His extended hand coiled into a fist. CLICK. CLICK. CLICK!

"I heard you won't be in school tomorrow." He said.

The clicking ceased. "It was the principal's idea." The woman lifted her head to face her son. She smiled lightly. "I wasn't going to say no to paid time off."

"Well," Kyle said. "You're certainly making the most of it." He didn't wait for a response before entering his room.

With a swift motion, he threw his bag onto the bed. He paused and let the resulting squeak circulate the room. Then he plopped into his chair, spun around twice, and selected another letter.

Dear Mr. & Mrs. ███,

I am truly sorry for your loss. I am a prison guard who on occasion patrolled Steven's cell. We shared a few brief conversations. During our talks, I learned two things. Firstly, he was quite intelligent. I regret the world never saw his true potential.

The second being the compulsion he had was simply his nature. The boy could not help what he did to those women, just as many of us can not help our own desires. Please do not blame Steven or yourselves. There was nothing either of you could have done.

In our final conversation, Steven confessed his greatest fear was dying without leaving a lasting impression. He believed this fear somewhat motivated him, although he confessed to wondering if he had the potential to make his mark in a different way. I shared with him the same opinion I'll share with you. I believe he had the capability for more, but the compulsion was simply too strong.

In the end, Steven was confused and didn't want the world to judge him. I can certainly relate. I've spent the better portion of my life feeling confused and fearing the world's judgement. I remember tucking my young son into bed wondering what he thinks of me and wondering what he would think if he could live inside my mind. These are fears many people possess. I believe that is why Steven never tried to contact you. In his own way, he was trying to protect you.

Mr. & Mrs. ███*, I hope this letter brings you some peace of mind. Steven was a dapper and intelligent young man. Though many will view his actions as evil, I assure you they were not a reflection of his whole character. I am confident you were supportive and loving parents. That is your true legacy. I wish you the best and will keep you in my thoughts.*

Yours Truly,

A Friend

Kyle sighed and emitted a long continuous stream of air before rereading the letter. There was something about this letter that troubled him. It was eating at him, festering like a tick, but he couldn't place his finger on it.

The letter was underwhelming. His father clearly didn't connect with Steven as much as Trevor. Disappointing? Yes, particularly after struggling through an agonizing school day awaiting it. But was this unsettling? No.

Why did it say Steven couldn't help himself? Was his Dad defending him? Was he trying to make the parents feel better? Kyle banged his fist against the table and grunted in aggravation.

Something else was off. What was it?

Instinctively, he opened his phone. Jake's number was the first to appear in his recent contacts. His finger wagged over the call button for a moment, then retreated. He turned to face his bed and imagined Jake sprawled out on it. He'd be on his stomach and face the foot of the bed. His chin would be propped on his forearm, allowing him to be eye level with Kyle.

"It's me right? Or is this letter messed up?" Kyle would say.

"Did you expect death row letters not to be?" Kyle didn't actually know that's how Jake would respond. He did, however, know that after speaking Jake would flash sly grin. Kyle would shove his arm, lightly. Then Jake would ask to read the letter.

Kyle decided to do the same. This time he paused at the line: *I remember tucking my young son into bed* . . . That would catch Jake's eye. "It's kind of weird he wanted some convict's folks to know this," Jake would say. Kyle stopped reading and let Jake dissolve into the crevasses of his mind. That was it!

Kyle closed his eyes and tried to visualize the scene but couldn't. He could envision his father; the still image was forever burned into his mind's retina. Yet he couldn't picture him by his bedside. In fact, he couldn't even see him in his room. That man never tucked him into bed.

He could see his father's face with ease. His facial features were as sharp as if he were standing before him, but that was it. He had heard his dad's voice, but he had trouble associating it with the man he remembered. He saw his father as a still image. He didn't move or talk.

Kyle recalled a memory of going to the park with his parents. His mother sat on a bench and beamed as she watched her son conquer the swings. Every aspect of her face, from her hair to her cheekbones seemed to bounce with excitement.

He knew his father was there. He couldn't recall seeing him, but he could hear him. It was the only time he could remember the voice and the man together; the low, raspy breaths the man took in rhythm to Kyle's swinging. Like clockwork, Kyle would swing towards the sky before returning to earth. He'd feel pressure on his back, hear the grunt, and then repeat the process. Kyle closed his eyes and listened to the grunts. His breaths began to mirror the low rasp. Before long, he imagined it was their sheer force alone that propelled him up the swing.

The night his father left, Kyle's mother had tucked him into bed. She had kissed him on the forehead and whispered, "Goodnight my little warrior." By the feel of her lips, Kyle knew something was wrong. Typically, they were warm and damp. That night they had only been cold.

Kyle then focused on his mother. He could no longer see her on the park bench. He tried to visualize her in a different setting, but the only thing to materialize was the image of an aging woman in a sticky nightgown sitting at the dining room table. She had her head tilted and was gazing wistfully at the apartment door. It was as if she expected it to open and her husband reenter her life.

Kyle cringed as he pictured his mother fidgeting with

the box lid. THAT DAMN BRASS BOX! She kept it by her bedside for a year after he left, and now it was back. He continued to imagine her cocked head staring longingly at the door, while her fingers continued to caress the tin memory.

***

Tammy and Jake sat facing one another. An empty chair sat between them. It was extended from the table, as if hosting some invisible force.

Jake methodically sipped his milkshake while Tammy fiddled with her wristband. They were in their customary table at the coffee shop. They appeared to be some of the only customers and the chatter from the kitchen seemed unusually quiet.

"Those dead letters are interesting," Tammy said, breaking the silence. Jake nodded, and Tammy continued. "I can only imagine what Kyle must be going through."

"That's why he's so upset, right? This shit with his father." Jake said. The image of Kyle's raised finger and hardened face still burned in his mind.

Tammy shrugged. "It probably has something to do

with it."

"What is that supposed to mean?"

"It means he has a lot going on right now." Tammy sighed, "can we not talk about Kyle right now?"

"Then why the hell do you keep bringing him up?" Jake caught sight of Tammy's expression. "Sorry," he meekly added.

"It's ok," Tammy said. She took Jake's hand and lightly smiled. She wore tight jeans and a slightly baggy sweater. She sported a wider frame, but her clothes accented it well. By all accounts, Jake knew she wasn't an unattractive girl.

Tammy had worn something similar the night she and Jake became a couple. Jake was helping her with some math homework, a subject she admitted to struggling with. It all happened fast; the hands brushing against each other, the awkward silence, the kiss . . . Tammy had asked if they were a couple. Jake hadn't objected.

Tammy just had to tell Kyle. She couldn't keep her mouth shut for just a couple of days. In fairness, she didn't know about Kyle's dad at the time. Would that have stopped her? Jake knew he should have stopped her. He replayed that moment, wishing he had just cupped his hand over her mouth.

But he didn't. Jake let her explain in detail about how it was what both he and she wanted and how it wouldn't affect their friendship. All the while, Kyle remained stoic. He gave the perception of maintaining eye contact, but Jake knew otherwise. Kyle's gaze had been focused on the dead center of where Jake and Tammy were standing. He was staring into the distance somewhere, trying to concentrate on something else, anything else . . .

Kyle's deadpan expression consumed Jake's thoughts. It wasn't the true Kyle. The true Kyle was the one who glided under the suspended red and orange lights of the Halloween fair. That had been the last night Jake saw Kyle smile; when they rode The Midnight Madness.

"When you're racing down that first drop, the adrenaline takes over," Kyle had said. "You can say whatever you want; it's pure instinct. And no one will know what your instincts make you say. They'll just hear your screams." Jake suspected Kyle was smiling when he spoke, but he couldn't know for sure. Kyle's back had been to him.

Jake had pondered Kyle's words during the ride's incline. He turned to Kyle, but he appeared lost in his own thoughts.

When they had reached the top, Jake felt nauseous. He swallowed the vomit in the rear of this throat, just before they took the plunge. The extreme velocity vibrated through every vein in Jake's body. During which time, he had opened his mouth and screamed "Tammy and I are dating."

Judging by Kyle's face, he hadn't heard Jake's confession. At least he could say he had told Kyle first. Jake wondered if Kyle said anything during the drop. If he did, what was it?

When the ride came to a stop, Kyle had smacked the handle bars and laughed. That was the moment. The moment he smiled. When he was happy, the world bore witness to the flawless warmth held between his lips.

"So, you'd like to?" Tammy asked. Her fingers had

transitioned from her wristband to her milkshake straw.

"What?"

Tammy exhaled. "Would you like to go out tomorrow," she reiterated. "Like a date?"

"Sounds great." Jake continued to sip his milkshake. He looked past Tammy and stared at coffee shop's entrance. He tilted his head. Wistfully, he continued to stare.

***

Tammy eyed the girl sitting next to her. She and the boy to her rear were exchanging notes on a loose-leaf notebook. They didn't seem to notice anyone or anything else as they passed the notebook and whispered to one another.

Tammy didn't see why they needed to do both. She couldn't make out what they were saying, except when the girl said, "Draw it again, I'm not that fat." Tammy adjusted her posture and slightly sucked in her stomach.

When class was finished she checked her phone; no new messages. She opened her last conversation with Jake:

Do you want to meet at the restaurant or would you

prefer I pick you up?

He hadn't replied. The iPhone app told her that the message was read at 9:37PM yesterday evening. They didn't have any classes together, but he'd probably be waiting for her by his locker. They'd been meeting there recently. She quickly constructed another message:

Looking forward to tonight! I'll wear the red dress you like.

She inspected it for a moment and decided it was too formal. She replaced *forward* with *4ward*, added a 'wink face' at the end of the second sentence, and then she pressed 'Send.'

Tammy placed the phone into her hand-me-down purse. She paused for a moment, then she pulled the phone out and placed it on silent mode. It made her less anxious to not listen for a reply.

She left the classroom and directed herself towards Jake's locker. When she rounded the first corner, she found herself almost face to face with Kyle.

Uncontrollably, she gasped. He looked equally surprised for a moment, then to her surprise his lips curled slightly upward. "Hey," he said.

"Hey Kyle." There was a pause. "Ho- How has the dead letter reading been going?"

"Pardon me, madam, but I haven't the faintest idea what you are referring to." He spoke with a British accent.

Tammy squinted for a few seconds, then realization dawned on her. "I'm afraid you're suffering from a memory lapse." She said, also in the British dialect. She, Kyle, and Jake spoke this way from time to time when a new topic was introduced. The formal English accent appeared, and the topic was dropped; no questions asked, no answers given.

Tammy smiled and spoke in her regular voice. "Well if your memory ever returns and you want to talk, you know where to find me." Kyle looked like he might object, but then he nodded.

Satisfied, Tammy walked past Kyle to finish her mission. "Tammy," Kyle said. She stopped and turned around. "The other night," He continued. "When you and Jake were over, I didn't mean . . ."

"Pardon me good sir, but I haven't the faintest idea

what you're referring to." Her English accent resurfaced. After those words, and a shared laughing eyeroll with Kyle, Tammy turned and marched onward.

She wore the same smile on her face until she reached Jake's locker and found him nowhere to be seen. She fumbled through her purse and retrieved her phone; no new messages.

***

When Kyle returned home, he was pleased to see his mother was not in the kitchen. The brass box was there, but she was nowhere to be found. When he approached the table, he discovered a note that said, 'Out for groceries.' He checked the refrigerator and realized that besides food and other necessities, they were also out of beer.

Kyle returned to his room and selected another letter. Just before he opened it, a thought struck him. He wasn't sure what triggered it, but for some reason he wanted to know the last time he and his dad spoke.

He didn't say I love you. He never said "I love you" to his father, at least not after he left. Actually, he couldn't remember his dad ever saying it to him either. Kyle stared at the envelope in his hand. If his dad had known he was going to die, would he have written Kyle a letter?

Without another thought, Kyle opened the third forgotten letter of the dead.

Dear Mr. & Mrs. ███ *,*

I know this is a difficult time for you. I am a security guard who was assigned to Dalton's cell. I knew your son very well. Dalton was not like many of the other inmates. I saw inside of him a great passion I know the world will never forget.

He had nothing but respect and admiration for both of you. Mr. ███ *, Dalton told me that you are quite the poet. I recently purchased one of your works and can say I agree. Mrs.* ███ *, Dalton spoke volumes about your gift for the piano. While I have never heard you play, his enthusiasm was proof enough. More than anything, he talked about how happy your visits made him and how much he truly loved you two.*

During our many conversations, Dalton revealed that he planned the assault on those men due to the many bigoted comments they made regarding the color of his skin. While I can never condone taking a life, I truly sympathize with Dalton's situation. My partner and I have experienced hate speech and know the damaging effects it has on someone. Over time, it can make you feel like you are not even a person.

It is my firm belief that Dalton's actions were the result of his environment and not his character. Please know that I experienced firsthand the kind soul your son had. I wish you all the best and will keep you and Dalton in my thoughts and prayers.

Yours Truly,

A Friend

Kyle cautiously placed the letter on his desk. The sound of the paper scraping against the wood seemed to ring in his eardrum. He sat motionless, listening so intently he could hear the hand of his clock tick with each passing second. Kyle listened to approximately 324 of these ticks until, with no prior indication of doing so, he stood up and left the room.

***

Kyle's face reflected no emotion. Like a frozen lake, it was desolate and permitted no entry. The only exception being his eyes. They hastily scoured the letter, combing it from top to bottom. With each reread, the eyes narrowed slightly more.

The ring of his cell phone broke the silence. Kyle's reaction was uncustomary for the situation. His expression remained constant, and his eyes didn't shift from the letter to check the caller's identification. By instinct more so than free will, he answered.

"Kyle," the voice was abrupt and held surface-level excitement.

"Hey Tammy."

"I just wanted to check in, in case you wanted to talk."

"Thought you were going to wait for me to call?"

"I did, but I have plans this evening. I didn't want you to call and think I was ignoring you."

Kyle sighed and smiled softly to himself. "Thanks Tammy."

Kyle heard muffled background noise, which led him to believe Tammy was fidgeting with something. Finally, she spoke. "Just because I'm dating Jake, doesn't mean I care for you any less."

Kyle didn't respond. A sharp crash erupted from the hallway. Kyle hung up the phone and followed the rumble of screeches and grunts. When he reached the bedroom, his mother was on her knees digging through the drawer that had been ripped from her nightstand.

Scattered papers and bent family photos shrouded the floor. In the middle of it all lay an open, now slightly dented, brass box. Kyle knew what the box contained. There was only one picture of his father in the entire house. Kyle had seen the picture only twice. The first time being when he was eight.

The picture depicted a man of average build, cradling a young child wrapped in a blue-silk blanket. The man's shaven face sported piercing green eyes, thick glasses, and a full engaging smile.

A noise not unlike nails against a chalkboard echoed through the room. Kyle realized his mother was scraping her fingers against the jagged wood at the bottom of the drawer.

"Mom," he said firmly.

The noise stopped. The drawer fell from the woman's grip, as her stare connected with Kyle. His image burned within her glassy eyes. She staggered forward. "Where is it?"

"Where is what?"

"You know damn well what." She slurred through clenched teeth. Her breath reeked of cheap beer. "Where did you put it?"

"I don't know what the hell you're talking about."

The woman struck her son's face with an open palm. "Tell me where!" She raised her hand again, but Kyle seized it and forced it down.

Following this exchange, his mother burst into tears. "I'm sorry." She pressed her face against her son's chest. "I'm so sorry."

Upon looking down, Kyle realized her hands were bleeding.

Cautiously, he guided her to the bathroom. There,

he washed and bandaged her wounds. When the bleeding had stopped, Kyle walked his mother to her bed. He covered her body with a warm blanket and adjusted the pillow ensuring she wouldn't sleep on her back. He remained by her side until she fell asleep.

***

The knock was light at first. Midway through, it abruptly overcorrected itself mimicking the roar of thunder. With his mother out of commission, Kyle was the designated doorman. He reached the knob in time to prevent another thunder roar. Jake stood before him, dressed in dark, belted, pants and a button-down shirt. His hair was gelled and slicked backward, exposing his pale forehead. There was a brief silence before the two exchanged a breathy "Hey."

Without another word, Kyle moved towards his room. Jake followed at a safe distance. "You look nice," Kyle said just before reaching his door's archway. "Did you have plans tonight?"

"Nothing too serious."

"Date with Tammy?"

"Told her I'd be late . . . What's up? You sounded upset when you called." He cautiously sat on the edge of Kyle's bed. There had existed a time when Jake felt comfortable enough to plop on the bed and chat with Kyle about any conceivable topic. There was a time when that bed was his oasis. Now mere contact with the cushion caused Jake's armpits and back to perspire.

Kyle walked to his desk and picked up his father's most recently read letter. "He was a faggot!" His tone had suddenly shifted to rival the knocking.

"What?"

"My father, see!" He shoved the letter in Jake's face, his thumb feverously pressed against the line. "My partner and I experienced hate speech . . ." Kyle said in a mocking tone. Before Jake could finish reading, Kyle ripped the paper away and slammed it on his desk.

"Maybe he was talking about a work partner?"

"Oh sure." He shook his head then pointed accusingly at the letter. "What kind of straight guy talks like that?" He stomped across the room, then turned to lock eyes with Jake. "You don't think I know a faggot when I see one?"

Kyle's words strapped Jake in place. They vibrated around him and shook the room with the force of a 300-foot drop.

Jake's chest tightened. He was once again descending the rollercoaster. Adrenaline was pouring through every fiber of his body, but he was numb. He was numb when the coaster had come to a stop and Kyle had smacked the handle bars. Then under the safety harness, visible to no one else, Kyle had taken his hand.

Jake suddenly realized the moment of truly freeing adrenaline didn't come during the fall, it came after. He drew in air, exhaled, and returned Kyle's glare. "I thought you didn't like that word."

"And I thought Tammy wasn't your type." Jake remained stoic. He appeared to be biting his lip, though his mouth hung slightly agape. His face hardened when Kyle began to cry.

"I burned it," Kyle said. He continued without waiting for a response. "Mom had this fucking picture of him. She looked at it every day. All this time, she thought she was the reason he left. But it was him! He left us for someone else."

"Us?" Jake said. Kyle never included himself among those his father left behind.

"Fuck him! The only people he cared about were murderers." He paused for a moment. "Fuck her too! She can waste her life mourning a faggot who never loved her. She . . ." Kyle could no longer form words. Tears streamed down his face and lingered on his chin.

Jake stood. "It's ok," he whispered. Kyle shut his eyes and squeezed his temples between his thumb and index finger. "It's ok," Jake repeated in an even softer, but somehow confident, whisper. He held Kyle's hand and pulled it from his trembling face. Gently, he removed Kyle's glasses. The boys' lips reunited.

Neither Kyle nor Jake knew how long the kiss lasted. Neither knew what would happen after. But they both knew it wouldn't be forgotten.

A Bluebird's Song

The teacher slipped his finger in the tight space between his neck and his shirt collar. He tugged on it twice in a failed attempt to secure some more breathing room. He stood by his desk. Although he was young, the top of his head was beginning to bald. He was tall, so he often stood to conceal his thinning line.

In a few moments the first day of the teacher's new Psychology class would commence. The teacher had lots of energy and frequently gestured while speaking. For this reason, no one suspected he was actually disappointed the majority of his class was populated by Freshmen.

In the final seconds before the class period began,

the teacher took a quick survey of the room. The room was filled mostly with young white girls, though there was some diversity. He noticed one African American student and a few boys were in the back. Among those boys, in the very back corner by the window, sat David.

The teacher had not yet met David, so he had no way of knowing that it was unusual for the boy to be paying attention. During most classes, David spent his time either staring out the window or reading one of his books. David was an avid reader, but only read things that interested him. Included were works of literature, scientific studies, and the occasional ballad. Not included were essays, word problems, and most text books.

The teacher also had no way of knowing that, unlike most of the other Freshmen who took the class only to satisfy a humanities credit, David actually had a genuine interest in the subject. To the veteran reader, the human mind has the enticement of an unopened book.

With the last of the straggling students slipping through the door, the teacher began his lesson. "How many of you have had a dream? And I don't mean a dream of becoming president. I mean the event that takes place while you are sleeping that allows you to experience the impossible."

Some of the class looked confused, but many responded by raising their hands. The teacher continued with an added amount of excitement.

"Dreams are often doorways into the subconscious. They are also the subject of much debate. Some believe dreams are merely a jumbled collection of random thoughts. Others think dreams are more like untold stories; that they express the hidden desires, motives, and emotions of an individual."

This gathered David's attention. Often he had fantasized about writing his own story. He held such an appreciation for the words of people like Harper Lee and J. D. Salinger. They were performers, creating an interpretive dance with their words for the world to see. People like that were able to entertain with both creativity and an expression of themselves.

The teacher continued to explain the assignment. "For the next two weeks, each of you will keep a dream journal. It's important that you keep it close to you anytime you think you might sleep. That includes daytime naps and math class." The class laughed. "Most dreams are forgotten by an individual only a few minutes after they regain consciousness. So it's imperative that you all record your dreams as soon as you wake up. I'll give each of you the chance to share your favorite dream with the class at the end of the two weeks."

To the students, the teacher appeared to have an answer for everything. One girl said she didn't ever dream. "Everyone dreams." The teacher spoke with enthusiasm. "Most people dream between four to seven times a night. However, the amount of sleep you get will usually determine if you will remember them. Dreams tend to be remembered if they occur during REM, or deep, sleep."

Another student asked if her not remembering her dreams meant that she wasn't sleeping well.

"It's possible. Though it could be that you have never really tried to remember or analyze your dreams before. We will discuss it in more detail in two weeks."

The teacher took a moment to gently tug his neck

tie. He walked to his desk and held up a pile of papers. "Tonight I want you to read this short article about dream symbolism. This individual analyzes a dream in which he dreamt he was a bluebird."

When David returned home, he spent the better part of an hour searching for the notebook his mother gave him for his birthday. It was a hardback red leather-bound notebook with tassels hanging from the front cover. He had considered it far too proper for regular classwork. Upon finding it, he stroked his hand over the cool spine. He opened it to find at least two hundred blank lined pages. He pressed his nose to white surface. It had that new book smell.

At bedtime, he eyed the journal cautiously before placing it on his nightstand. It was normal for the boy to read 20-30 pages of one of his books before drifting to sleep. That night, however, David didn't read. Instead he went almost immediately to sleep. The first thing he did when he woke was record his dream in the leather notebook.

I was shopping at a local Food Lion. I had no memory of how I got there or even what I was looking for. I remember spying a bluebird in the distance. Its wings sounded like they were playing an instrument I wasn't familiar with. I followed it into the 'Canned Goods' aisle. I was looking at cans of soup when my sister Lisa rushed to my side. I turned to face her, but when I did she was no longer Lisa. She was now my cousin Kevin. However, I didn't seem to notice the change.

"You need to find some tap shoes?" He said.

I told him without actually speaking that I didn't know where tap shoes were.

"Then find someone who does." By the end of the sentence, Kevin was again Lisa. This character shuffle proved to be the norm for the remainder of the dream.

It's difficult to exactly describe what happened next but I will do my best. As soon as Lisa/Kevin finished saying those words, a young man appeared. I'm not completely sure, but I feel like there was even some music to fit the occasion. The kind that plays right when the hero is introduced in a movie.

I don't know what this man looked like because his features were constantly changing. The only thing that remained the same was his shaggy jet-black hair. It looked exactly like Lisa's boyfriend's hair.

I asked if he knew where I could find tap shoes.

"Tap shoes are too good for you." He said in a somewhat mocking tone. "Just look at the shoes you wear. Disgusting. Especially those laces."

Suddenly Lisa/Kevin was enraged. "Don't you dare insult his laces!" she/he screamed. Despite this one outburst, there was no real indication that these two beings were going to engage in any sort of physical altercation. Still, in the next moment, the two were rolling on the ground punching each other. The transition skipped all of the build-up. The fight had no start, it just was.

I turned in what I assume was an attempt to find someone to help. There was not another living being in the entire store. When I again looked at Lisa/Kevin and the young man, they were no longer fighting. Instead, they were embracing. I won't go into detail but they were, for lack of a better term, all over each other.

As with all his entries to come, David dated and titled his work. This dream was named 'Tap Shoes.'

David continued to sleep with his leather notebook and a ball-point pen within reaching distance. Sometimes the dreams he recorded seemed to coincide with his day. One night he watched The Slumber Party Massacre with his family and dreamed about the movie. In his dream, he alternated between being the cool girl Trish, the heroic outcast Valerie, screaming party goers, the killer, a bluebird resting on the windowsill and even at one point the killer's drill. He appropriately titled it 'Slumber Party Nightmare.'

Other dreams, were less relatable. One in particular involved David peacefully walking down the street. He sang alongside a passing hummingbird and allowed a bluebird to mount on his outstretched arm. In the next moment, he was hiking up a mountain. Then he was in the desert. Next came the snow, ocean, an active volcano. The scene continued to change although David himself seemed undisturbed. The sequence finally ended with him suddenly appearing in his room, where his anxious mother and a man he at the time assumed to be his father (though in hindsight the two men looked alike) informed him that he was late for his dance recital.

Mondays were a known symbol of misery amongst high school students. David was the exception. He glided from place to place, fueled by the excitement of his weekend dreams and the connections they brought. During lunch, he took a seat in the cafeteria. As had become his routine, he sat directly across from the skinny boy with thick glasses who was seated beside him in Psychology class. The two sat with a fairly close proximity to other groups of students, but with enough distance to keep their conversations strictly to themselves.

"Have you had anything to write in your journal?" David asked the skinny boy.

"Do you think this is too bruised?" The boy held an apple. He appeared to be examining it with mild scrutiny. Unsatisfied, he removed his glasses and squinted at the fruit.

"Yeah it looks fine." David gave his friend enough time to set the apple down before attempting to continue the conversation. "But Gerald, I want to know if you've written anything in your journal yet."

"Journal? Oh, that dream journal thing?"

"Yeah, have you written anything in it?" His anticipation was beginning to show.

"No. I'm about to make something up. I don't dream."

"I actually read that we all dream. We just don't remember unless we wake up before it's over."

The skinny boy didn't answer. He was chewing a bite of his apple. He appeared to be hesitantly chewing, as if still concerned over the fruit's quality.

"I'm saying you don't need to make something up. Do you keep your journal by your bed? It helps to write your dream down as soon as you wake up."

"I guess . . . Why do you care so much?" The boy said, now slightly annoyed.

"I don't care that much," David said. "I just mean

some of the dreams have been, you know, inspiring. Like, the other day I had this weird dream that my sister was sort of in."

"You have a sister?"

"Yes, Lisa. You know I do."

"I've never seen her."

"She's older. She lives about an hour away. But I know I've mentioned her. Hell, I remember you meeting her."

"I haven't."

"Whatever, the point is that the dream had a guy that looked kind of like her boyfriend. And the two of them . . . Well, I just decided to call her this Friday and it turns out her boyfriend had proposed to her the night before."

The skinny boy, somewhat more amused, looked up from his food. "So you're psychic or something?"

"No, I'm saying I wouldn't have called my sister if it weren't for the dream. I was the first one in my family to know she was engaged, and because I called she decided to bring her fiancé by the house the next day."

"Did you tell her about the dream?"

"Not over the phone. I was going to tell her in person, but she was too busy talking to my parents."

"Your Mom probably found your dream interesting. Isn't she some kind of artist?"

"She didn't say much about it. Ever since the engagement, Mom and Dad have had trouble talking about anything other than wedding plans."

"When is the big day?"

"They haven't decided yet, but that's not important."

"It's kind of important. It's your sister's wedding."

"I know it's important, but what I'm sayi . . ." His words were interrupted by a sudden shriek. The boys and about half the cafeteria shifted their gaze to a girl who had just spilled milk over her pink lacy dress. By the time she calmed down, the skinny boy had returned to examining his apple.

David found that he dreamed more than the average person. Almost every night he had at least one dream to record. They were always in such strong detail as well. He'd never given much thought to his subconscious. Before he hadn't seen their importance.

Although most of his dreams were interesting to a degree, he still planned to share the one about his sister. He felt it held more weight than the others. This continued to be his thought until just two days before the dream journal was due.

It began as a normal day of Psychology class. The teacher was explaining the reading homework. David wasn't really listening. Ever since the assignment, he spent most of his class time skimming his dream journal (which now had forty pages filled with dreams and real life connections). When he wasn't skimming, he took pride in dragging his fingers limply over the tassels on the leather covering.

David didn't do the reading homework. He didn't even remember what the assignment was. He didn't intentionally ignore the teacher; his excitement was simply too great. Today, though, things were a little different. When Sally Greywater asked about the 'Bluebird of Happiness,' his curiosity was intrigued.

David was still at the point where he hadn't developed a lasting attraction to any member of the fairer sex. He did, however, secretly decide that if he were to be attracted to a girl, it would be Sally Greywater.

"Bluebird of Happiness . . ." the teacher began. "The majestic bluebird has been a symbol of happiness since before your great-grandparents were even born. Centuries ago Xi Wangum, a fearful and immortal goddess from China, used the bluebird to deliver messages. Later, many people started looking at the peaceful creatures as a representation of the sun because it gave them hope."

The man stopped and gazed out the window as if expecting to find a bluebird perched on the looming tree branch. Unsuccessful, he turned to his students and continued the lecture. "Even in today's society, many famous artists have used the bluebird as a means of expressing joy. Sandor Harmati, Paul McCartney... are just a few examples of people who have made songs to immortalize the bluebird."

The next morning, David awoke suddenly. He

snatched his journal and hastily clicked on the light. He gave his eyes only the minimum amount of adjustment time, before he began writing.

I knew it was a hot day. People left trails of sweat on the cement as they passed my lemonade stand. I tried to advertise my product, but the words wouldn't form. I seemed to be incapable of speech, or even opening my mouth for that matter.

A woman in a sombrero walking an anteater caught my attention. I watched the beads of sweat pour from the sombrero almost like a waterfall. Suddenly I noticed the gray-haired man. I only looked at his face because somehow I knew he was naked.

"Would you like some lemonade?" I asked with my power to speak returned.

"Do you happen to have a bluebird's song?" He spoke with a British accent.

I shook my head.

"Would you mind checking the house?"

I didn't see his hand, but I could tell he was pointing

behind me. I turned around to see my house. My first house. The one my parents had when I was born. I hadn't seen it since I was five, but the image was clear. It was a two-story brick home, with four evenly spaced windows on each floor. A small staircase and porch led to the front door.

I walked across the long yard. The further I walked, the further I seemed to get from the door. I began to feel sad. Every blade of grass I stepped on felt important. It was like I was crushing something, but I didn't know what.

Somehow, I reached the stairs. I started to feel a sense of fear as I climbed them. Something waited for me beyond the door. I could feel it . . .

Unable to give the entry a proper ending, he simply titled it 'The Closed Door.'

The dream had a weird impact on David. The other dreams in his journal seemed to reach some form of conclusion. 'The Closed Door' did no such thing. Something about not knowing what was on the other side of the door captivated him. It pestered David like an itch that can't be scratched. He remembered someone telling him that they often had dreams like his. Unfinished products that later repeated themselves, sometimes with an ending.

Perhaps for those reasons, David chose to share 'The Closed Door' over his original choice 'Tap Shoes.'

When the day came to produce his work to the class, David's body experienced strange phenomena. His hands twitched. Not his fingers, but his hands. They vibrated as if they were planted on a running dryer. This occurred all day. He experienced it when attempting to eat his breakfast and while trying (and failing) to grasp his pencil in his morning classes. Inside, he didn't feel nervous. His pulse didn't race and he drew breaths in rhythm, but his hands painted a different story for all who came within arm's length of him to see.

It was a relief when Psychology class started. The teacher straightened his back as the students took their seats. Once everyone was situated, he instructed them to take out their dream journal projects.

"Who would like to begin?" About one-third of the students raised their hands and teacher pointed across the room. At first David thought he was pointing to Sally, but then the girl who sat in front of her stood up.

Jasmine was the only African American in the classroom. She made eye contact with only her journal as she read two sentences about how she dreamed she was a doctor on her favorite television show.

"Very good. Let's give her a hand." Most of the students clapped. David didn't.

"Who's next?" This time the teacher pointed directly next to David.

The skinny boy with thick glasses took his turn standing before the room. Contrary to Jasmine, he read without looking at his journal. David noticed that his friend's journal only consisted of a few pieces of loose-leaf paper and a paper clip.

The skinny boy began to share. "So in my dream, my mother and I went to a store. At first, we thought it was a grocery store, but they sold dogs. So we bought a dog and took it home. Then I started to do some math homework, and this dog started talking. He told me how to solve my problems. He said he was Albert Einstein in a dog's body."

David doubted the dream's authenticity. Yet again,

the dream was praised. Again, the class clapped.

David stretched his hand higher. The teacher appeared to take notice. His finger seemed to reach all the way to the back of the room and tap David's desk. "Go ahead, David." The teacher said, confirming his selection.

David didn't remember standing. He didn't remember opening his journal. It was possible he had always been standing with the journal open. The journal twitched with his hands. His eyes moved rapidly to keep up with the shifting text. His speech competed with his eye speed.

His words spewed one after the other in rapid succession. He tried to slow down but he only seemed to gather speed. In only a few seconds, he had reached the part about the grey-haired naked man. The dream itself flashed before David's eyes. Sweat ran down his forehead. The sun burned the back of his neck. He remembered the man. He saw only his face but he knew he was naked. The man's lips moved. He could hear the words coated in the heavy accent "Do you happen to have a bluebird's song?"

"I'm going to stop you there, David." The teacher

spoke with a satisfied grin. "Who else had at least one dream involving a bluebird?" Almost every student raised their hands. The teacher gestured his pointer finger, taking a brief count. "Splendid. For the past two weeks I have provided homework and in-class assignments involving our feathered friend the bluebird. By doing this, I subconsciously influenced you to dream about the bluebird. This is a technique called *priming* and it is what we will be covering next."

David was still standing. His open journal was twitching in his hands. The teacher was beginning a lesson on priming. The other students were taking notes. David eventually sat down. No one clapped.

The teacher loosened his collar once class was dismissed. He did so while keeping David in his sights. The boy didn't leave the room nor give any indication of even vacating his seat. After giving David what he deemed an appropriate amount of time, the teacher approached his student.

"May I help you with something?" He took notice of

the boy's hand. David held it limply over a closed red leather notebook. It appeared to tremble.

"You said dreams are like windows into the mind… stories waiting to be told."

"I said they could be."

David continued to stare at his notebook and shaking hand. "Was this whole dream journal and subconscious exercise just about teaching priming?"

"No, but the subconscious is very complex. Dreams are just a fragment. Not to mention their interpretation is vague. Professionals are still divided on whether they think dreams actually have a real world meaning."

"But do you?"

"I'm sorry?"

"Do you believe dreams can mean something more?" David finally looked at his teacher. His eyes now seemed fixed on him.

"Of course! I wouldn't assign the journal if I didn't."

Suddenly more energized, David picked up the leather book and extended it towards the teacher. "Would you read my journal?"

The teacher took the book and held it on the palm of his hand. Mentally, he appeared to weigh it. "How many pages did you say this was?"

"I'm not sure. I had lots of dreams and thoughts about them. You could tell me what you think? If you think there is something more?"

"This certainly is impressive." Quickly, the teacher sat the journal on David's desk. I wish I had the time to give this the attention it deserves, but unfortunately I don't. Now, I'm sorry to tell you that I need to lock the classroom."

David picked up his journal. He stood and walked to the front of the classroom. He made it halfway to the door before he stopped. He turned around and threw the journal at the closed window.

***

It was a little before noon when Sandra's doorbell rang. Without looking through the peep hole, she flung the door wide open. A look of disappointment momentarily crossed her face when she saw it was a delivery man.

"Morning Ma'am." He said with a slight southern drawl. "I have a package here for you."

The woman took the package. After glancing at the address label, she quickly put it by her side and did her best to ignore its existence.

"I need you to sign here." The man handed Sandra a clipboard.

"Thanks." Sandra signed her name in what was essentially a single cursive letter with a line attached.

The man whipped the sweat from his forehead and let it drip from his fingertips onto Sandra's porch. "It sure is a hot day, isn't it ma'am?"

"It is." She handed the clipboard back to the man and smiled without using her teeth. Quickly, she shut the door before he had time to utter another sentence.

Sandra spent the rest of the Saturday inside. She sat the package on her kitchen table and tended to the day's errands. She mopped the hardwood floor, shampooed all three of her rugs, and cleaned the one and a half bathrooms. After that, she took two scoops of chocolate ice cream for her lunch break and then returned to work. She found the windows needed washing and the tables needed dusting.

Unfortunately, by six-thirty the small house ran out of chores and Sandra was left tending to the mail. She put the package in the seat of a kitchen chair, out of sight. Sandra then sorted the letters. The ones addressed to her and her alone, she put in a pile. She dedicated the remainder of the evening to opening/reading them individually. Even the junk mail, she opened and read word for word.

The phone rang at approximately ten after seven. Eagerly Sandra checked it. However, upon realizing it was her mother, she finished the sentence she was reading before answering.

"Hello."

"Hello Sandy. This is your mother." The old woman always introduced herself despite Sandra having caller ID.

"Hey, Mom. What's up?"

"Oh I just wanted to check in."

"Well thank you, Mom. I'm doing fine."

"Good . . . good . . ." There was a brief silence. Although she tried to mask it, the old woman's voice stuttered slightly when she next spoke. "So how's Davy?"

"He's not coming back, Mom."

"Don't be ridiculous." The old woman laughed. "It's only been a couple of days."

"Five days," Sandra said. "Five days since I've talked to him, six since he left."

"Oh that's nothing. When your father and I first married, he pulled this same stunt. I didn't see hide or tail of him for two weeks. Men go through this sort of th . . ."

"Mother."

"Sandy, listen to me. I was telling your father this was a definition mid-life crisis. What with him quitting his job and that ridiculous talk about teaching dance. He just needs a little time to clear his head. You'll see. If anyone asks, just say he's out of town. It's not a lie, I assume he is . . ."

"Mother," Sandra repeated. She managed to perfectly imitate the tone the old woman would constantly use to convey her annoyance. "He sent me a package."

"Well what's in it?" The old woman didn't attempt to hide the anxiousness in her voice.

"I haven't opened it."

"Why not? Honestly Sandy, if you are so convinced that Davy isn't coming back then why aren't you taking things more seriously?"

"Mother, if he wants to leave, then me opening a box isn't going to do a fucking thing to change that."

There was silence. "Well . . ." The old woman eventually said. "Just give it some time dear."

Sandra exhaled until she didn't think there was any air left in her lungs. "Thanks, Mom."

"Of course, dear. And remember, this is your business. You don't need to tell anyone until you are absolutely sure of what's happening."

"Will do, Mother."

"Goodbye dear. I'll call you again tomorrow."

"Bye."

After hanging up, Sandra threw away the junk mail and turned her attention towards the package. She reasoned to herself that if she didn't open it, she would be subjected to more scolding tomorrow.

The brown cardboard box was small, but somewhat heavy. When she emptied its contents onto the table, a red leather book fell out. The book featured a pair of elegant looking tassels and had a large bend in its spine. She picked it up and continued the examination. It felt cold. The first clump of pages looked worn and the others untouched.

When she opened it, she recognized the handwriting instantly. She flipped through page after page of her husband's work. The detailed accounts of his dreams, the pages dedicated to explanations and theories . . . She felt a sudden rush come over her as she read. It was like a cold chill except it was somehow warm at the same time.

When she got to the entry, something caught her eye. It was dated only a week ago. All of the other entries were dated fifteen years ago. The other works looked old and cemented in the pages by time. The final entry was different. It looked fresh and neatly presented with all the words lining together.

It was titled: 'The Open Door.'

I knew it was a hot day. People left trails of sweat on the cement as they passed my lemonade stand. I tried to advertise my product, but the words wouldn't form. I seemed to be incapable of speech, or even opening my mouth for that matter.

A woman in a sombrero walking an anteater caught my attention. I watched the beads of sweat pour from the sombrero almost like a waterfall. Suddenly I noticed the gray-haired man. I only looked at his face because somehow I knew he was naked.

"Would you like some lemonade?" I asked with my power to speak returned.

"Do you happen to have a bluebird's song?" He spoke with a British accent.

I shook my head.

"Would you mind checking the house?"

I didn't see his hand, but I could tell he was pointing behind me. I turned around to see my house. My first house. The one my parents had when I was born. I hadn't seen it since I was five, but the image was clear. It was a two story brick home, with four evenly spaced windows on each floor. A small staircase and porch led to the front door.

I walked across the long yard. The further I walked, the further I seemed to get from the door. I began to feel sad. Every blade of grass I stepped on felt important. It was like I was crushing something, but I didn't know what.

Somehow I reached the stairs. I started to feel a sense of fear as I climbed them. Something waited for me beyond the door. I could feel it.

Once I entered the house, I discovered the inside wasn't the same. There was no staircase ascending to a second floor. The ceiling was low and rooms narrow. In the dream I still thought it was my parent's house, but once I woke I was able to recognize it as my current home. The rooms were all the same but my wife and all the furniture were missing. In their place seemed to be some sort of dark mist.

I felt compelled to walk through the dark shadows. As I moved, I heard a strange sound. It didn't sound like it was coming from a bluebird. Perhaps a woodpecker? It was almost like a knock in rhythm to my steps. When I gazed at my feet, I discovered I was now wearing tap shoes.

The place I now called home was hollow. There was no singing bluebird for me to find. I advanced from empty room to empty room. All the while, the only sound came from my shoes. Clicking.

The Smell of Ripe Oranges

Every spring my family peels oranges in the meadow. This year is no exception. With backpacks full of fruit, we leave. The short walk is made long by the sun. Mom has to stop twice for a 'short water break.'

The sun is right above our heads when we reach the fresh green grass. We sit in a circle. I smile for the first time in weeks as I take in a deep breath of the spring air. We open our bags to the smell of the fields of Florida.

I peel the first orange. It splits into five even pieces. I take one for myself. I hand one to my little brother who eagerly puts it in his mouth. I put one next to my sister, she is struggling with her half-peeled orange. I give one to my mother. She wipes her eyes before thanking me.

I place the last piece in the spot where Dad used to sit. He always loved the smell of ripe oranges.

Perchance to Daydream

The water danced around my ankles as my feet made contact with the muddy surface. Most of the liquid landed on his pants. He didn't care. Neither of us wore rain jackets. The precipitation trickled down our smiling faces.

"You call that a splash," he said.

I bowed my head and wrung some water out of my mane. Then I flipped my hair back and let it fall damply against my neck. "It was bigger than yours."

"Then I guess we need to go together." He took my hand and we dove into the next puddle.

In that moment, I couldn't hear the rain. The world was silent.

***

On our one-year anniversary, I took my boyfriend, Scott, to my parents' beach house. Our anniversary fell in late October, a time when only local home owners dared expose their flesh to the frigid sand and paralyzing ocean.

I preferred the solitude. During the Fall and early Winter months, the humble island was how I remembered. It wasn't until Valentine's Day that the tourists began flooding the shores with their boisterous music boxes and discarded beer cans.

"Are you sure you want to be alone?" Scott asked. He placed his hand on my shoulder.

I wriggled free before he could squeeze. "I won't be long." I said. I fastened the new helmet and mounted the rusty bike. "Just save me a spot by the water."

Scott and I met online. Some friends told me to try virtual dating. "You need to meet someone, Rachel." They said. "It's fun, like you're exchanging a hundred love letters in one day."

Scott's first sonnet consisted of a single question:

"So what is it you are looking for?"

Given my inexperience in the area, I had previously opened a google search entitled "How to Respond in Online Dating." A quick glance at my computer told me the appropriate response was 'Friendship . . . Then maybe more . . .' I noted the repeat usage of the triple dots.

I was halfway through typing the words when I paused, deleted the message, and responded with "I don't know . . . You?"

Within a few minutes, he replied "Friendship . . . Then maybe more . . ."

My response, "How to Respond in Online Dating?"

Almost instantly, I received "You caught me" and a sideways smile.

I remember staring out my bedroom window. I imagined the man in the photo (tall, dark haired, a slight belly) sitting hunched over his monitor. His walls would have no picture, but there would be an antique clock somewhere. Like me, he'd have a window, but only one. He'd glance out the window and run his hand methodically through his peach fuzz trying to construct his next reply.

The thought made me smile. That smile led to dinner, and that dinner led to another . . .

Scott was a gentleman, but not overbearingly so. He paid for the first date, but didn't argue when I paid for the second. Still, I never shook the feeling he was combing through our conversations with a check list. "I've been working as a Communication Specialist since I graduated college." I said during our first in-person meeting. *Age Appropriate: Check! Educated: Check! Stable Job: Check!*

Scott proved himself to be nice. I waited months for the curtain to fall, but it never did. Perhaps that's what was so infuriating.

When I invited him to the family beach house, he insisted on staying awake while I drove. For half a day I was held captive by his continuous questions and hourly pats on the shoulder followed by "How are you holding up? Do you want me to drive?"

It was like he was afraid of silence. He, like so many southern suitors, feared a woman with a wandering mind. I drove the entire way, getting less than 3 hours of sleep just to spite him.

I didn't understand Scott's desire to lay on the beach. The weather was too cool for him to actually enjoy himself. However, I had no problem with it. The last thing I wanted was for Scott to accompany my bike ride. I needed the silence. I didn't want to talk about Jason.

I told Scott Jason died on the island. I didn't consider it lying. Jason loved the beach. I figured a rock could crack a skull just as easily here as anywhere else. Besides, his ashes were spread across the island's dunes. It's what he would've wanted.

My brother would've given anything to speak at his own service. "The doctors said it took 10 seconds for this to be fatal." He would lift his hair for all to see his battle scar. "Let me tell you, those were some long seconds."

I don't remember crying. I'm sure I did, I just couldn't visualize it. However, I could see Mom. Her face was smeared with bodily fluids when the pastor approached us. "It is a shame to lose someone so young," he said.

To me it was the opposite. Jason was forever

immortalized in his youth. Our grandfather died a year before Jason. Most of his friends had already passed. Those that were alive for the funeral talked about visiting him in the nursing home saying "He looked so happy until the end."

When my time comes, I hope people have more to say. I shuddered. It was because of the wind, I think . . . Then I briefly recalled stumbling across my first grey hair a couple months ago. I plucked it, even though I'm not supposed to. "Now you've fucked yourself," Jason would've said. "The whole lot's going grey now." He'd hold his knee and rock back and forth, laughing regardless of whether others joined.

Jason left this world a perfect specimen; our memories never tainted with years of shriveling skin and mental decay. Well, perfect may not be the correct word for Jason, but youthful certainly was.

Even Jason's pictures looked perfectly preserved. His body seemed almost photo shopped in the family portrait next to his casket. His clothes and skin were just a touch brighter than that of the people he called family.

Mom, Dad, and I blended together with our bland stares and dark hair, while Jason distinguished himself with his blonde curls and toothy grin.

The funeral was 10 years ago. That meant I was now almost 7 years older than Jason.

When I left the house, I noticed a fellow rider in front of me. He was too far ahead to make out anything other than a vague outline of his back. It looked like he had a destination. I decided to follow.

We rode on the main street for a few minutes before the rider suddenly veered left. He appeared to go down a street I didn't recognize. My brakes howled with years of accumulated arthritis when I shifted into the turn.

"Old piece of shit" I said.

The bike sat in our shed for years accumulating rust. It was a 12th birthday gift for Jason. I had wanted a bike for months and received a coloring book, Jason never even asked for one. His birthday cake was blueberry. I remember the berries smashing against my fingers when I threw it to the floor.

Mom and Dad sent me to my room. When Jason came to visit, I was angry. He wasn't. His touch was gentle yet effective. He slowly guided my chin until my eyes were level with his. It was done without words. I never told him, but it helped.

Jason wouldn't have liked my job. There were nice people and good pay that came with a career in communications. That wouldn't matter to Jason. Sometimes I think he only went to college for the parties. He always talked about dropping out and retiring to the beach. "I'm going to build things, and you're gonna help, Rach." He said. "You think it, I'll make it!"

My brother knew better than anyone I was a daydreamer. The window was my best friend in school. It about killed me that my office didn't have any. I was so accustomed to sitting next to the smooth glass. Throughout my education, even extending to particularly boring college lectures, I caught myself gazing out into the exposed world.

If the sun was shining, I imagined the kids cutting class and basking amidst its glow. The wind made me picture the struggling house wife attempting to hold her groceries against the breeze. Though my favorite was the rain.

When water trickled down the glass, I imagined myself dancing. I'd be dancing in the cool liquid. The world seemed pure, while the smell of precipitation infused my lungs. Sometimes Jason was there, daring me to splash in one of the many puddles. I'd close my eyes and twirl, while the droplets flowed through my hair.

These daydreams always ended the same. In a flash, I'd be snapped back to reality. The pouring moisture, replaced by a teacher's glare or parent's scolding finger.

The road was very linear, with no visible end. It was surrounded by plots of land. The plots were composed of red mud, and divided by wooden planks and thick wires. It was exactly what the island didn't need, another conventional neighborhood.

Don't get me wrong, I love new buildings. Growing up, the island gave birth every year to unique houses and their extraordinary owners. Jason's favorite was the cat lady. The house featured bridges, treehouses, elevators (to this day, I still have not figured out how the cats operated it), and many more amenities designed for the feline visitors. Like its owner, the house always had a cat crawling over it somewhere.

My favorite was Adrian's house. That probably wasn't his name, but he was a surfer and the title seemed like a good fit. His house was three stories tall, but only in the back. The front of the house was one story, the middle was two stories, and the rear was three stories. This upward progression created an incline. The roof was designed with a unique slant which gave the entire house a wave-like appearance. It was the perfect place to meditate before catching a big one.

Now, however, some contractor got together with some accountant and decided it was more 'economically feasible' to build matching rectangular houses. Almost all the new homes sported this new structure. Besides color and window placement, there was nothing to distinguish them.

After a few miles, the endless stretch of pavement

broke into a right turn. It was then I began to notice my fellow rider. He stood on his pedals when he rounded the curve, letting the wheels veer just slightly into the turn. Jason always rode that way.

The distance between us rendered him blurred. I squinted. The similarities became more noticeable. The dark sweat pants, the black hoodie . . . Jason always bundled himself no matter the temperature. Mom would chastise him for coming home with clothes drenched in his perspiration. "Why can't you look outside and see it's t-shirt weather?" She always said.

However, today wasn't t-shirt weather. For a pedestrian, I'd classify it as long-sleeve temperature. But coasting along on the rust-bucket bike amplified all of the day's less desirable traits. The wind howled against my exposed flesh and stung to the bone. I pressed my chin into my jacket and pushed forward. As I grew closer, I noticed the rider's face was cloaked in a hood.

I knew it was impossible, but the image of me catching the rider swam through my mind. He would pause for a moment, then turn around and unhood to reveal his curly blonde locks. Perhaps he wouldn't recognize me. Or maybe he would proudly guide my hand over his victory scar? It was possible he would look different. He skin could be darker. His hair might be shorter, maybe a different color. I didn't know what was going to happen, but I knew I needed to see him. The desire burned through me. It seemed to be the only thing that kept the blood pumping through my veins.

Just as I was closing in on my target, I averted my gaze long enough to notice the building. It stood alone as the first of many to occupy the future neighborhood. For the time being, the doors and windows were mere open holes in the otherwise unblemished house. A construction truck was parked in the front yard, though it looked unattended. As with the other homes near the shore line, it rested on the support of several large wooden stilts. Unlike the other homes, this one had a deformity. A gaping hole in the building's right indicated a large ocean-view window room. The kind where the tinted glass encompasses the entire wall. A passerby sees the window's color and design, while the owner sees out into the world.

I imagined the glass exterior would soon be covered in a red coat. That would allow it to contrast well with the palm grass the new owners would surely plant. Then again, it was possible they would tint the window blue. Then it would match the reflecting ocean.

As if done by my own will, the mystery rider stopped before the development. I approached cautiously, using the heel of my foot instead of the rusted brake. He stood before me now, only a few feet from my grasp. His shrouded face fixed on the unfinished structure in what I somehow knew was admiration.

That was it! Jason recognized the house was unique. He had to stop to admire it; we had to admire it. He wanted me to stop. I needed to stand beside him. We wouldn't touch or do anything to acknowledge his return. We'd just stare at the house and discuss the kind of person who would make it their home.

The sheer adrenalin may have been why I didn't notice. But standing in the shadow of the premature home, I finally recognized the small frame of the mystery rider. That, and the bright pink shoes. I never put it past any man to wear pink, but Jason wouldn't be caught dead or undead in pink, light-up sneakers. I felt a peculiar mixture of deflation and relief.

I could see Jason mocking me for thinking he was some girl in a hoodie. I continued down the road. I didn't bother looking for her face, I didn't see the point.

I couldn't help but envy the rider girl. She was so concentrated on the house that she didn't notice the woman stalking her for the past 3 miles. Growing up, the endless possibilities of the construction site would've fascinated me to no end.

When I was 10 and Jason 14, he took me to a similar house. The island was fairly uninhabited then, I'd only ever seen a couple of homes under construction. "Come on," he said, running up the un-railed steps. My brother was always eager for whatever life threw his way. It was as if I imagined a life for myself, but he lived it.

Once inside, he ran around the convolution of floor boards like a puppy inspecting its new home. "See that," he said pointing to an arrangement of wooden bars stacked in a row. "That's going to be the door. This is all one room!"

Then in a flash, he ran to the backyard balcony. I remained in stationary awe. It was so much space for such an empty room.

I ran the scenarios through my mind. I decided the open entrance would be a living room. The owner was an aging English professor, so the walls would be filled with book shelves. A fireplace would mark the center where two angled arm chairs sat on opposite sides of a rounded table. He was unmarried, so the extra chair served as courtesy to his few, but regular visitors. I imagined him of average build, with a greying beard and half-moon spectacles. A large window would be in view of the chair, so that on stormy nights he could listen as the rain would splatter against the glass.

I'm not sure if those were my exact thoughts. In hindsight, they seemed a bit detailed for a ten-year old. Still, that's how I remember the day; the first of many adventures we took exploring the island's unfinished homes. I also remember feeling nervous when Jason left me alone in the large empty room. Thus, I decided to follow him onto the balcony.

When I reached Jason, he was standing on the balcony's edge. He beamed at me. His fingers were folded over the bridge of his exposed penis. In the moments before I adverted my gaze, I witnessed his urine spew over the intended back yard. My eyes were forcefully shut, but I could still hear the fluid crackle against the soft ground.

What was most disturbing was not the act itself, but the fact he was proud of it. "This land is mine now," he said. "That's the law of nature." Though I've never admitted it and shall never until the day I die, that is the picture I see when I remember my brother. Not the entire image, just his face; the elongated grin of pure satisfaction while his cock is cradled beneath his sweat stained armpits.

The flame that once crackled for the mystery rider, now burned for the road. I had to know where it ended. I let countless identical plots of land transcend to blurs in my corner eye. My main focus was on the miles of rubber to be burned by my wheels.

Ahead, I saw a tree whose branches crossed in the

middle forming a sideways 'X.' It seemed a fitting endpoint for my journey, but it was only a landmark. The road stretched on. I could tell it was leading to more.

A younger me would've stopped for the tree. I'd prop myself against the jagged bark and slip into a daydream. Concealed under the branches yielded the prime location to see not what the world was, but it could be. As I let the bark and leaves fade to a blur, I would think about the mystery rider and how I'd mistook her for my brother.

I didn't actually think she was Jason, but I had hoped for something . . . different . . . different than a young girl. I contemplated what was wrong with me. I missed Jason. I always did, especially when I visited the island. But this was different. I hadn't felt him this strongly in years.

I thought about what made this trip different. *I'd been to the island before: Check! I'd pulled all-nighters before: Check! I'd ridden his bike before: Check!* Then I knew . . . I'd never been to the island with anyone other than Jason and my parents; no distant family, no friends, not even another boyfriend. I'd allowed an outsider to invade our territory. The island had always been the place where

Jason and I could escape the rest of the world. We'd splash in the rain and daydream about our future, because we always had time for a future. Now I had all my future boxes checked courtesy of . . .

"Damn it, Scott!" I spoke these words aloud and smacked my forehead. I'd been on my journey for at least a couple of hours and forgotten all about him. All this time he had been waiting for me.

I could see Scott laying half naked on a beach towel obsessively checking his watch. It was too cold for that, but he would do it because it was expected. His chalky urban body would flinch in the breeze, but that wouldn't stop him. He'd put on a show for all to see. Complete with an open umbrella and two unfolded chairs.

Anyone that looked in his general direction would hear about his wonderful, but ever so tardy girlfriend. "She's on her way. She's just exercising as usual." No one could think he was by himself. They all needed to know his relationship status.

He always had to check those boxes. He came on this trip because he wanted to be supportive. He offered to drive because he wanted to be considerate. There was always a reason for what he did, but he never allowed himself to just feel what was right. Not that I wanted him to, but he'd certainly never piss off a balcony.

I remembered when I told him I was considering changing jobs. The check list encompassed reason after fact about why Communications is "an appropriate stable occupation for someone at my stage of life."

Did he ever consider that: *I'd done the same job for over ten years: Check! That I'd never been given a promotion or accolade: Check! That I was bored: Check! Check! Check!!!* . . . Shit . . . now he had me doing it.

It was abrupt. Just as I had caught myself in a daydream, I found myself being snapped back to reality. I had reached the end.

I don't think I dismounted, yet somehow, I was standing next to my bike. Finally, after hours on that rusty bike battling the October wind, I'd crossed the finish line. I stood, clenching the squeaky handle brake in my fist, staring into . . . nothing.

There was absolutely nothing. No houses under construction, no 'X' shaped tree, no anything. Even the road ceased to be. The blend of gravel and tar was clean cut leaving only a few feet of dirt before a murky ocean.

Why would someone pave a long damn road if it was going to end like this? I stayed on the path. There were countless distractions, but I never stopped. And this is what I got? At the very least, there could've been a patch of land cleared for one last abnormal house or a turn-around circle, so the surrounding area had potential to one day be a cul-de-sac. I laughed in my head. There's not even room for a fucking turn-around circle. There was absolutely nothing, the path just ended.

A tear dripped down my check. I'm not sure why.

The ride back was longer. The wind was with me, but it wasn't fanning any flame. Images of Scott shivering on the sand and growing cobwebs in my windowless office loomed over me. I thought a few weeks ahead to my birthday. I was almost 36. Soon, another year of my story would pass on by.

"When did my life become a checklist?" I said aloud. It was a good thing Jason wasn't here. One look at my life and he'd crash his motorcycle all over again. "Why wear a helmet?" He'd say. "There needs to be some thrill."

I'd checked all the boxes. The only thing left was for me to reach the end of my road. Check!

In the distance, I saw a familiar figure slowly progressing towards me. I had no desire to see her. I couldn't take it. The smooth skin and youthful eyes would be the final blow to permanently extinguish what was left of my flame. I lowered my head and kept my pupils focused on the bits of gravel disappearing beneath my spinning wheels.

I was almost past her when a force I couldn't explain took hold. I could almost feel a hand gently raising my chin until I was eye level with the other rider. Her face was tattered in age spots and the silk-black hair I imagined was tucked under her hood was withered grey. With her flashy pink shoes and shiny new bike, the elderly woman continued her way to the finish line. I thought about telling her the road was going to end, but suddenly realized she wouldn't care.

As our paths crossed, I admired every precious wrinkle on her dried face. When her eyes made contact with mine, I saw something strange. They were soft and tainted with crow's feet, but there was a glimmer buried beneath the cataracts. A twinkle I had only seen when I thought of my brother.

I raised my hand to wave. Her crackling jaw seemed to mouth the word "Hello."

I came to a screeching halt as I reached the 'X' tree. I pushed any thoughts of the windowless work prison and Scott's pale chest away. I settled beneath the unfolded branches and felt the bark massage my back.

As my eyes began to close, I took a final glimpse of my fellow ridder. Her blurred silhouette faded against the setting sun while she was slowly pulled towards the road's end. I clung to the possibility, no matter how slight, I might awaken to find myself splashing in a puddle.

The whole world silent, while the rain danced through my hair.

24s Hours

"24 hours," he hissed. The smell of his rancid breath curled up my nostrils and lingered even after he disappeared, leaving behind a ring of blacked ash.

Standing alone in the abandoned churchyard, I felt as empty as the bones below my feet. Rage began to consume me. *Why had I come here alone? Why did I have to go at night? I could have waited until Sunday to pray for my child at a functioning church, like a normal person.* I pounded my head as if to beat out the answers.

Some would say I was blessed. I saw an angel. An angel from Hell. Now I had one day to choose somebody, anybody, for that wretched creature to drag straight to Hell and rip apart their soul. If I refused, he would take me.

I drove home under the pale light of the full moon. I couldn't, as a Christian, condemn another to such a horrific death. I accepted my fate quickly. There was no use ruining my last day on Earth.

The next morning, I called in sick to work. I took my wife and son to the finest restaurant in town. Afterwards, we went to the paintball court. We watched our boy on the "battlefield," easily outmaneuvering kids twice his age. His smile was intoxicating.

"Why are you rewarding him?" My wife asked. "He is supposed to be grounded."

It all seemed so small now. The arguments with my wife, the discipline notes from teachers, my boss refusing to pay me the respect I deserved . . . Those weren't the important parts of my life. I took her in my arms and kissed her like we were again on the alter saying our vows. "I love you," I said. I stroked her confused face until she smiled and kissed me back.

At night, I tucked my boy into bed. I ran my fingers through his curly hair, before kissing him goodbye. The drive to the abandoned churchyard felt long and short at the same time. I began to contemplate my fate. I was a good, Christian man. *Why did I deserve to die when there were murderers and dictators at large?* This curse could be a blessing. I could rid the world of a psychopath.

Once again, I found myself standing before the beastly monstrosity. This time, I stood confident. "Do you know who in this world will kill the most innocent people?"

He nodded.

"I choose them."

"Very well." His smile was familiar in a way that made my skin crawl. "You will be spared." Without another word, he was engulfed by amber flames.

I fell to my knees. Relief washed over me. *I was safe! Not only that, I was a hero! I just saved countless lives.* Then, my phone rang. I answered it and greeted my wife cheerfully.

Her voice was frantic. "Our son is missing!"

When I returned home, I saw his bed was surrounded by a ring of blacked ash.

Flying Freely Over the Sea

December 10th, Freshman Year:

The service was formal. Though I didn't have a strong basis for comparison; a grandmother when I was three (I couldn't recall which side of the family) and an aunt I had meet twice in my life.

Five rows before me, a pastor spoke. Truly, I attempted listening to his words. Had they been more interesting, I may have been able to maintain concentration. However, much like the attire, flowers, and accompanying photographs, they reeked of normality. With only two exceptions, every detail seemed recycled from the regular heart attacks, cancers, and illnesses.

As the casket lowered into the earth, I focused on the first abnormality; the tombstone towering over the shoveled dirt. It rested fully engraved, awaiting its new occupant. Even with my limited funeral experience, I knew how uncommon it was to have a headstone fully prepared at the time of burial. My mind briefly considered the practicality of pre-funeral grave markers.

A strong wind blew through the evergreen tree needles. It was cold. The clouds were blackening as the sun was going down. The majority of people had retreated indoors. The reception would be starting soon, but I didn't care. I found myself staring at the unorthodox tombstone. A stone unfairly marked for a life taken prematurely. The stone of a friend that I was not ready to leave.

"Life is the most precious gift we have." The pastor's words rang in my subconscious; the only part of his speech I remembered and was incapable of forgetting. They seemed inappropriate for a suicide. I drew in a deep breath and held it until the pressure swelled inside my lungs.

"Oh Gale," I said. "How could this have happened?"

December 3rd, Freshman Year

"You looking for another bitch slap?" Chris asked. He was leaning against the wall for support. Three of the six buttons on his flannel were undone. However, he still possessed enough composure to emit sarcasm while simultaneously sipping what smelled like gin.

"I need to know where Gale is," I repeated.

"Probably getting to know some of the fresh meat." He hiccupped, then placed his hand on my shoulder. "You know, you don't have to be so stuck up her ass. There're other places you'd be more welcome." His hand lingered, then slowly rubbed down my arm.

I shrugged out of his grip. "I'm serious. You need to help me find her."

"Oh, I neeeeed to." He laughed, which caused him to lose his balance and slide further down the wall. "What'll you do for me if I do?" He parsed his lips and made two repeat clicking sounds.

"Fuck you." His smirk allowed me to quickly realize

my poor word choice. I made direct eye contact with him and hardened my face until it felt immobile. "Please help me."

With a decent amount of energy and some faint but noticeable grunts, Chris hoisted himself from the wall. His eyes narrowed and rapidly darted over my full body more than once. "Okay," he finally said. With a slight nod, he staggered away.

***

The veil of intoxication is a manipulative Siren. Now sober, the whimsical merriment of the night ceased to exist. Vixens who once seductively championed the dance floor, now morphed into half-awake floozies suffering mini seizures. Brave soldiers who previously battled the beer-pong table turned into sluggish bobbleheads swatting at invisible flies. The air reeked of digested alcohol mixed with morning breath. Even the music contorted from a rhythmic stimulant to a barrage of inconsistent shrieks.

The partygoers themselves became insufferable. When questioned about Gale's whereabouts, most merely tilted their heads and resumed dancing. As unhelpful as that was, it was worse when they did respond. "Coooooooolllin! I misssed you! You are like . . . literally . . . the nicest person ever," said the girl I once let borrow my pen in Chemistry.

"I seen you going man! I seen you going!" The towering upperclassman I did not know slapped my back. "You going hard man! I seen you, brother."

Around a quarter past one, I tried calling her roommate. No answer. Five minutes later, I tried Dwaine. I'm not exactly sure why, save a ride back to my room there wasn't much I expected he could do. Still, I felt the strangest compulsion to do so. I wasn't surprised when it went to voicemail. His phone operated like a solar clock; once the sun was down, it was down. It was an exaggeration, but only a slight one.

I searched long after the everyone else left the party. The alcohol-free hours felt like they were beating their way into my skull. It became impossible to determine if the pounding in my head was from the increasingly boisterous music or the onset of a hangover. Nonetheless, I couldn't really think about anything except my last words to Gale.

I had called her phone more times than I remembered. The only answer I received was static followed by a cheery "If you don't know who you've reached, you should hang up now! Otherwise, you can leave a message. Who knows, maybe I'll respond." I had to have left at least half a dozen messages. Looking back, I realize my priorities were illogical, but at the time I wanted nothing more than to say I was sorry. I knew I shouldn't have to apologize. Or at least I didn't have to admit I was completely in the wrong. But, I also knew it was what she needed. I didn't have to be right, but she could never be wrong.

My search ended up lasting over three hours and would have lasted longer if not for that phone call. I had answered my phone so quickly hoping to hear Gale. Instead, I heard Chris. He spoke coherently, indicating an infusion of water and time since our last encounter. By the serious and silent tone of his mildly slurred speech I knew something was wrong. Then he uttered the soft words "I found Gale."

December 2nd, Freshman Year

I spent the past few hours watching Dwaine paint in

the room. I tried to act interested in his work, but craved any excuse to vacate the premises. I didn't have the patience to be the artist he was. He would hold up a few of his works from time to time. I would try to smile and complement them, but couldn't generate words more constructive than "nice color" or "great detail." I knew he could tell I wasn't very amused. Perhaps that's why I decided to go with Gale when she showed up at my door?

Dwaine was holding up a painting with a lot of blue and yellow colors moments before the knock came. I worked on constructing a complement for what I would later realize was a beach under the morning sky. "I want you to have this one," he said.

"Me?"

I thought for sure I misunderstood. A smile with an accompanying nod informed me that I hadn't.

"Thanks, but I couldn't . . . you spent so much time on . . ."

The knock came, and I instinctively sprang to the door. Without even allotting me the time to stand aside, Gale strolled into the room. I glanced over at Dwaine, who appeared to shrug to himself and then returned to examining his masterpiece. "I'm not letting you get out of Chris's party," she said.

"You want to go with me?" Again, I thought I misunderstood.

"Who else would I want to go with?" Gale had avoided me for weeks, but somehow, she managed to impose stupidity upon me for even questioning her statement.

"Are you sure you want to go, Colin," Dwaine's voice echoed across the room. He was still intently concentrating on his portrait. Obviously, he was hinting at the Gale-infused agony I tormented myself with the past weeks. My response was quick, but it was a decision I would spend an eternity regretting.

***

Chris greeted us in the usual manner. He and Gale exchanged alternating air kisses complete with exaggerated sound effects. I received a real kiss, on the cheek. I scrunched my cheek and closed my accompanying eye at the embrace of his suction. It was a small price to pay for the free alcohol.

"Well," Chris said releasing my face and giving me a once over. He wore his traditional jeans; a runt when compared those belonging to classmates of proportional size. The first button of his flannel shirt was undone, giving air to the sparse hair follicles plastered on an otherwise pale and barren surface. "I see you brought some fresh meat, Gale. You're lucky I'm not a vegetarian." Chris stood aside, as always, and allowed us to enter.

The humble house read more like a game of Twister, thanks in no small part, to the multi-colored lights. Just like the game, every new color represented something different. Drinking games commenced under the blue light, the dance floor under the green, and make-outs under the red. Music radiated off every wall. Regardless of color placement, everyone seemed to be dancing. Chris handed me a beer. I offered Gale the first sip, but she was already chugging Captain Morgan.

***

Gale's breath was heavy and saturated with rum when I found her. She was standing under the light post by

Chris' driveway. Under the condensed illumination, I could visualize the rawness of her face. She clenched a plastic drinking bottle to her bosom.

"Are you ok?"

"Do I look ok?" I noted the tears budding in her eyes.

"How much have you had to drink?"

She threw her cylinder to the ground. "It doesn't matter how much I've had to fucking drink. He still shouldn't have done it."

"Who did what?"

"This fucking freshman. He kissed me. He kissed me on my fucking lips."

"Is that all he did?"

"All he did! I have a boyfriend. I have a boyfriend and he kissed me! And the way he did it. I fucking hate him."

A couple of late partygoers strolled past. They were exceptionally large and sported football uniforms. Catching the tail end of our conversation, they halted and peered in our direction.

Gale started screaming. "What the fuck do you guys want? Do you think this is funny?" I don't remember ever seeing football players run so fast.

"Gale," I said. "You need to calm down."

"Calm down! You don't even know what happened."

"Here," I picked up her drink bottle and tried to hand it to her. "You can tell me on the way back to campus."

She refused to even touch her bottle. "He had his hands all over me, Colin. I didn't even really see his face until it started to suck my lips."

"He grabbed you?"

"No, we were dancing."

"Wait, you were dancing with him?"

"Yeah, so?"

"Did you even tell him that you have a boyfriend?"

"Why does that matter? He shouldn't have kissed me."

"Oh my God." I laughed and shook my head. "You are such a piece of work."

"What are you saying?" Her stare could cut glass.

"You know, sometimes I wish I were a girl. I could grind on anything that moves and it'd be alright. A woman can violate your body as much as she wants because she doesn't have a dick, right? Sometimes you're a real . . ."

"Slut?"

"Bitch."

Gale gritted her teeth and moved into my face. This was the softest she spoke the whole night. "You're just saying that because you want to fuck me."

Before I could generate an equally appropriate response, a firm and concentrated pressure collided with my face. I didn't feel the full force until Gale had already stormed away. Liquid was on my palm. Originally, I thought it was blood, but realized later it was vodka. Gale's bottle had cracked in my hand.

November 21st, Freshman Year

Almost a week had passed since my excursion to Gale's bedroom. Neither of us had acknowledged the incident, and frankly I wasn't sure if Gale recalled it. Soon, I'd be home for the holidays. I wouldn't see Gale for a college eternity and lose any hope of allowing the bedroom events to resurface. My mind spasmed with questions and curiosities, the most stubborn of which being what Gale had meant by . . .

"You need to stop thinking about her," Dwaine said. He stood beside his bed, surveying the canvas, erectly perched before him. Though we digressed into conversation, his eyes never once left the pastel frame. "I know she's attractive, but . . ." He extended the final word and deliberately trailed off.

"She's more than a pair of tits," I said.

"I know, Gale's a nice person." Dwaine said, officially confirming the subject of our discussion. "You two are just different."

"Is she too wild for a wholesome boy like me?" I inserted a southern accent on the latter part of my statement for dramatic effect.

"If you could fly, what would you do?"

I sighed to myself. Dwaine was notorious for beginning what had the potential to be a serious conversation, and then digressing into some psychological exercise. His questions were always unique, but I'd come to expect their arrival. Dwaine, in harmony with many people in my life, had become predictable. Perhaps that's what attracted me to Gale: she was a constant mystery.

"Go cloud diving, touch the sky, race the birds . . . I don't know." I paused, looked down, then snapped my fingers. "Be the subject of your next masterpiece, 'Bird Boy!'"

"There you go," he said matter of factly. "Do you know what Gale would do if she could fly?"

I shrugged.

He picked up his thinnest paintbrush and dabbed the tassels with speckles of blue. "She'd escape."

November 16th, Freshman Year:

"That . . . That there's the key." Gale completed her 'sentence' then proceeded to loosen her neck muscles and allowed her head to vacillate from side to side. Without the support of my forearm, she'd surely be on the floor. Hell, without my support, she'd still be on the floor at Chris's.

I attempted her suggested key. In her current state I wouldn't be wise to rely upon her judgement. However, most all dorm room keys have a similar structure and the one she suggested bore a striking resemblance to mine. The tumbler clicked, and the door was open.

I glanced at my watch, it was a quarter past 1:00 am. The perfect start to an abysmal Monday morning. Gale took five stunted steps then collapsed onto her bed. One arm and leg dangled off the edge. She laughed when I hoisted her leg and arm onto the bed to join the rest of her.

"You think I'm a spaz, don't you?"

"I think you're drunk," I said.

"Colin, do you ever question if people will miss you?"

The change in her tone was so sudden, I questioned if I'd heard correctly. "What?"

"Do you think my funeral will be well attended?"

"You should drink some water."

"No, I'm serious."

"Me too."

She attempted to raise her head, but it only shrugged on her left shoulder. "That's the only way you know for sure. True friends are there after death does them part." She yawned, and I think hiccupped.

"Gale, have you thought about this a lot before?"

"Do you think pigeons can walk without bobbing their heads?"

It was a peculiar thing to say, but I'll admit I was a bit relieved the 'conversation' had shifted. "I didn't realize they bobbed." I said.

"They bob all the time!" Her head jerked forward for a few repeated cycles. I wasn't sure if she was attempting eye contact or providing an example. "Except when they fly." She yawned again. "When they're flying freely over the sea."

Gale appeared to be asleep. I had the sheet across her waist when something took hold of my leg. I peered down to see Gale's fingers encasing me. "You're so nice, Colin." She said. Her fingers massaged their way to my inner thigh. "And so hot." I caught the breathiness the final word. Her hand made contact with the outside lining of my crotch, which I'm proud to say was in presentable form. She dangled there for a moment, then lowered her arm. "But Freddy wouldn't like that."

She rolled onto her stomach and proceeded to expel air. If she wasn't asleep, then she was giving an Oscar level performance. I stood at the edge of her bed until my watch's little hand was directly on the two. During none of that time did she break her rhythmic breathing.

Eventually, I left the sleeping beauty. At the time, I concluded her rambling to be just that. After all, she hadn't even used the correct name for her boyfriend.

November 15th, Freshman Year:

I returned to my room to find Gale lying on my bed. She was on her back, gazing up at the tiled ceiling. She clenched a clump of her long unruly hair in her fist. She was dangling it over her right eye. It sounded rather absurd, but it appeared she was contrasting her raven hair to the room's bleached ceiling tiles.

Upon seeing me, her face became elated. "Good, you're finally here. Your roommate is too busy reading to talk to me."

"I talked to you," Dwaine said. He was sitting on his bed across the room with a magazine in hand. I hadn't noticed him.

"What are you reading?" I made contact with

Dwaine's eyes. My current strategy to bide Gale's affection was to not provide the instant validation she craved.

"A murder mystery this guy wrote," Gale answered.

"The story's name is 'Dirty Laundry' and that guy used to go to our school; Dr. Conner Mills."

That name sounded familiar. I briefly pondered if my older cousin Mallory knew him when she attended our university.

"That's cool," Gale said. "But now we need to get down to business. There's a party tonight at Chris's place and I'm not leaving without both of you."

"I think I'll stay," Dwaine said. He held the magazine into the air and drummed his fingers along the spine. "They take paintings too."

A soft smile crept across Gale's face. "Ok, you're excused." She sprang off my bed. "But the untalented people need to drown our sorrows in liquor. Right, Colin?"

***

"I guess I'll let you in this time," Chris elongated every other word. He stepped aside and handed us both a beer.

"You want to dance?" Gale said. I turned in time to see Gale take the hand of a blonde fresh meat and guide him to the dancefloor. There he stood while she grinded. The boy was a deer in headlights, simultaneously experiencing adrenaline and terror. I watched them in-between light sips.

Chris put his arm around my shoulder. "Women can be torturous." He said.

"I take it the same doesn't apply to men?"

He rolled his pupils to the corner of his eyelid as if seriously considering my query. Then he broke concentration and smiled. "Care to play some beer-pong? I'll be shirts, you be skins?"

October 10th, Freshman Year

I accompanied Gale for a stroll across the shoreline adjacent to our campus. I asked if Dwaine could tag along, I feared he was beginning to rot in our room. Without his canvas and the security of surrounding walls, Dwaine was noticeably less comfortable. His posture worsened, and steps appeared stilted.

Gale, on the other hand, glided with a spring in her steps that held the approaching Autumn weather at bay. During our journey, she whispered in my ear multiple accounts of liquor-induced skinny-dipping adventures. The smell of her strawberry lipstick was enough to keep me captivated.

Once we reached the boardwalk, I abandoned the pair to purchase some ice cream. I was in the mood for strawberry and Gale requested chocolate chip. I forgot to inquire Dwaine's flavor preferences, so I purchased vanilla; a generic and reliable gamble. I, rather skillfully, balanced the three cones within my two hands and made my way to the boardwalk.

When I returned, my friends were sitting on a bench by the water. Gale enthusiastically pointed at the skyline and I noticed Dwaine was smiling. Upon seeing me, Gale approached and took her treat.

"Thanks," she said. "Your roommate and I just had the best talk."

"That's wonderful," I extended my arm towards Dwaine until I felt the contorted waffle leave my grasp.

Gale devoured her cone with an untamed poise that captivated me. Every bite generated a perfectly formed crater. Her cheekbones extended slightly as she let the dessert melt in her mouth. As the sunlight radiated off her smiling face, I imagined the taste of chocolate chips mixed with strawberry lipstick.

Briefly I glanced in Dwaine's direction. His convex back gave his body the appearance of a lowercase 'r.' That, accompanied by his methodical and exaggerated chewing, led me to believe he was withdrawing the minimal amount of enjoyment from that ice cream. I supposed I should've asked what flavor he wanted.

My eyes reverted to Gale. She was certainly a fine girl indeed. Most girls of her status wouldn't give someone like Dwaine the time of day, much less complement his conversation abilities. She laughed, open-mouthed, exposing the chocolate-chips nesting on her tongue.

I turned to locate the source of her amusement. If the way to a man's heart was through his stomach, then the way to a woman's was through her funny bone. I'd solve the puzzle of her humor and make her laugh harder than her boyfriend ever could. But when I about-faced my eyes detected only an empty boardwalk, save a few pigeons walking our way.

September 7th, Freshman Year

The house was partially concealed from street view by the surrounding trees. That, accompanied by its proximity to campus, made it the ideal habitat for weekend parties. It was within walking distance, but just far enough away not to attract public security.

My roommate cautiously stepped through the doorway. His shoulders descended further towards the ground with each progressive step. As if I possessed a gravitational pull, Dwaine remained firmly at my side.

"Colin, you made it!" From across the room, a pair of bright eyes belonging to the friendly boy in my Journalism class waved me down. I ventured through the catacomb of 'dancers,' through the implementation of many unique body movements, and finally made my way to Chris.

Chris was leaning against the wall, next to one of the

most striking creatures I'd ever laid eyes on. She smiled, revealing perfectly placed teeth. While clenching Chris's hand in a welcoming fashion, I dissected her on the sly. Her long dark hair and thin lips gave an alluring mysterious quality. Her body position and mannerisms embodied the textbook definition of confidence. However, notwithstanding her external appearance, something about her figure seemed fragile.

"Colin, this is Gale." Chris pointed his thumb at the siren. With the introduction, I realized I'd misplaced Dwaine in the crowd.

I extended my hand, to which she laughed. "You weren't kidding. He is old school."

"At least he's cute." Chris said. Quickly I realized I wasn't the examiner. No, I was the specimen.

Gale grabbed my still extended arm. "Let's dance." She said. My hesitance must have shown. "Come on, I don't bite. Unless you're into that." She laughed again; fully satisfied she could amuse herself.

"Don't keep him too long," Chris said. "I got dibs on the next dance."

Gale tugged me away. "Relax," she said. "Chris hits on all the fresh meat." She paused. "It's what we call freshman."

When we were nicely mixed into the crowd, Gale took my hands and guided them to her perfectly defined hips. Then we danced. We danced for hours and talked for a couple more. I told her I was a budding communications major with dreams of being a broadcaster.

What she told me was a bit more impressive. Gale was a sophomore Psychology major. She'd traveled to every state in the country, "except for the boring ones," and despite taking no foreign language courses she was a self-proclaimed master of street Spanish.

* * *

On the return to campus, we detoured past the lake harbor. Gale admitted the adjoining lake and forests were the only reason she stomached this "thankless place."

When we reached the boardwalk, I leaned in to kiss her. I felt two fingers press against my protruding lips and wrench me backward. "Colin." She wagged her finger like a mother to a wearisome child. "I have a boyfriend."

December 10th, Freshman Year:

"Life is the most precious gift we have." The pastor's words rang in my subconscious; the only part of his speech I remembered and was incapable of forgetting. They seemed inappropriate for a suicide. I drew in a deep breath and held it until the pressure swelled inside my lungs.

"Oh Gale," I said. "How could this have happened?"

"I don't know," Gale said. "Dwaine had all of us fooled."

I reread the engraving one final time. The effort was futile. No matter how many times my eyes examined the stone, my roommate's name always appeared under the 'RIP.' With no words, Gale and I walked to the reception.

***

The spacious room was occupied by a humble, but dedicated crowd of mourners. Their names and shallow details failed to register on my radar. Though later, I recalled being one of the younger attendees.

Dwain's parents stood a few paces from the room's entrance. They greeted their guests with an acceptable amount of warmth given the circumstances. I'd met the couple during move-in day. They'd both worn sweatpants and glowing smiles. Neither of which were in their ensembles today.

Perhaps Gale would talk to them? After all, she found his body. Dwaine had been dead for hours by the time she stumbled into our room. She pilfered my keys during our altercation and said she was looking for me to return them. My phone call to Dwain still haunts me. Somehow, I'd felt the need to contact him at a quarter past one. Maybe he was already dead when I called? Maybe not?

I studied Dwain's parents a moment longer. It astounded me just how much the man resembled his son. I veered my attention to the mother. Her glassy eyes stared just beyond the faces belonging to the hands she shook. Her mind was elsewhere, but for politeness she attempted focus on those offering their condolences. It was a look with which I was well acquainted. I gave it time and again when Dwain told me about his artwork. Without warning, the woman's forlorn eyes made contact with mine. The attention was so direct, I almost gasped. Instantly, I turned my head.

What captivated my attention next was the funeral's second abnormality. A brilliant mesh of blue and yellow colors perched on the room's central table. Dwain left no will. Had he, the beautiful illustration of a beach shrouded under the morning sun would've been mine.

The painting seemed to emit a familiar gravitational pull unique to me. Without realizing, I'd been drawn across the room and was standing inches from Dwain's masterpiece.

"It's beautiful," Gale said. She'd apparently been caught in the same vortex.

"He tried to give it to me." I said. "I don't think I gave it a second glance before now."

There was a silence. Finally, Gale spoke. "A bird flying freely over the sea."

"What did you say?"

Gale extended her finger and pointed to the upper right corner of the artwork. There, layered in obscure colors was the outline of a solitary flying creature.

"Dwain told me about this piece. He said no one notices the pigeon at first glance." She closed her eyes and snickered to herself. "He must've loved pigeons. He once asked me if I ever noticed how they bob their heads when they walk."

I cried following her words.

I shut my eyes and let the liquid stream down my face. I felt the warmth of Gale's hand as her fingers intertwined with mine. We would date off and on until she transferred schools at the end of my Sophomore year.

However, I wasn't thinking about my future with Gale. At the moment, I was soaring through the blended sky of a beach under the morning sun. I stretched my feathered wings, casting a shadow on the artist below. He was just off the shoreline depicting my pose.

The first time I met Dwain, he said hello. The last time I saw him, I couldn't remember if I said goodbye.